THE SEX

The woman untied the belt of her coat. With a wriggle of her shoulders the garment fell to the laboratory floor. Beneath, she was stark naked.

Critchlow gazed in disbelief as he took in the flawless beauty of her body. Her skin was creamy and unblemished, her breasts full and heavy. She exuded a tangible aura of raw sex.

'Who are you?' he said in a dry croak.

The woman's lush lips parted in a smile, her hips undulated as she walked towards him.

'You know who I am, Professor,' she breathed. 'I'm every wet dream you've ever had . . .'

Look out for other titles in the Sex Files series:

File 1: Beyond Limits – Carl K. Mariner
File 2: The Forbidden Zone – Nick Li
File 4: Double Exposure – S. M. Horowitz

Unnatural Blonde

John Desoto

**HEADLINE
DELTA**

Copyright © 1997 John Desoto

The right of John Desoto to be identified as the Author of
the Work has been asserted by him in accordance with the
Copyright, Designs and Patents Act 1988.

First published in 1997
by HEADLINE BOOK PUBLISHING

A HEADLINE DELTA paperback

10 9 8 7 6 5 4 3 2 1

All rights reserved. No part of this publication may be
reproduced, stored in a retrieval system, or transmitted,
in any form or by any means without the prior written
permission of the publisher, nor be otherwise circulated
in any form of binding or cover other than that in which
it is published and without a similar condition being
imposed on the subsequent purchaser.

All characters in this publication are fictitious
and any resemblance to real persons, living or dead,
is purely coincidental.

ISBN 0 7472 5730 2

Printed and bound in Great Britain by
Mackays of Chatham plc, Chatham, Kent

HEADLINE BOOK PUBLISHING
A division of Hodder Headline PLC
338 Euston Road
London NW1 3BH

Unnatural Blonde

ONE

SILICONE MERMAID, 60 MILES SOUTH-EAST OF MIAMI, FLORIDA. JULY 12TH. 2.20 PM.

There was no warning. No spluttering, which might have indicated a blocked fuel line or an intermittent electrical fault. The twin Yamaha diesel inboards simply cut out together, as suddenly and as completely as if someone had thrown a master switch. The prow of the thirty-eight-foot motor yacht *Silicone Mermaid* continued to carve a faint 'V' through the surface for a few more seconds then sank wearily into the unnaturally flat and lifeless Atlantic waters. Without even a slight swell to lap against the sides of the craft, the sudden stillness and quiet was striking, almost eerie.

Carl Scheller cursed, slamming the ball of his hand against the rim of the wheel, thinking of the six hundred bucks he'd shelled out for a full service only two weeks previously. His anger swamped the faint sense of unease which prickled in the back of his mind. 'Goddamnit, that's all I need. Fucking Florida grease monkeys.' He stepped back from the wheelhouse, craning his neck to glare up at the flaccid, shroud-like sails, unruffled by the slightest breath of wind. His frustration peaked, then started to dissipate as he remembered his nineteen-year-old passenger. He licked his fat lips thoughtfully, juicily. There were always compensations.

'So whadda we do now?' the girl in question whined, from somewhere behind him.

Scheller repressed a faint shudder as the coarse and nasal Bronx accent hacked through the silence like a rusty saw blade. He turned towards the girl who stood at the top of the companionway, her ripe lips pulled into a pout and her big baby-blue eyes regarding him sullenly.

He ignored the question, knowing that it was rhetorical. For all its youth and apparent innocence, there was a world-weariness about the girl's pretty face which suggested a premature cynicism, if not maturity.

'Stupid damned broad,' Scheller thought to himself. 'What the fuck do you think we do now?' His mouth curled into a leer.

Marylou Vacarro's vacant expression hardly changed, although her eyes dulled slightly with mute acceptance. Of course she knew the answer to her own question. It was a situation she'd been in a hundred times before. Dates had been running out of gas or experiencing ignition failure in remote places ever since high school. So why should Scheller be any different, even if he was old enough to be her grandfather? To confirm this diagnosis, if such confirmation was necessary, she became aware of the man's greedy eyes running lasciviously up and down her bikini-clad body.

'You think maybe we oughtta call the coastguard or somethin'?' she grated lamely, feeling that she ought to put up at least a token resistance.

Scheller frowned patronisingly. 'Listen, babe – do me a favour and cut with the lame-brain suggestions, huh? In fact, just keep quiet altogether. You're so much more attractive when you keep your goddamn mouth shut.'

Or when you've something filling it, he added to himself. And he had some ideas on that score. He moved towards the top of the companionway, stepping down the short flight of stairs and seizing her arm as he passed. 'Come on, baby – let's go below.'

Marylou acquiesced with a faint shrug. She had learned by bitter and sometimes painful experience that it didn't pay to resist the inevitable. She let Scheller pull her down the steps into the cabin.

It was small, and strictly functional. There was an icebox, a CD player, a cocktail cabinet and a bed, where two single bunks had been converted into a double. Scheller headed straight for it.

Dropping Marylou's arm, he threw himself down on his back, spreading his legs across its full width. He looked up at her, a humourless grin on his face.

'Well don't just stand there, honey. Let's see what you got under that bikini.' The grin turned to a scowl as the girl hesitated. 'For Chrissake – you didn't think I picked you up to take you on a honeymoon cruise, did you?'

Dumbly, Marylou reached up behind her back and unclipped the clasp of her bikini top, letting it drop. Slipping the skimpy panties over her rounded hips, she shook them to the floor, stepping out of them.

Scheller's eyes gleamed, taking in the youthful splendour of her firm body. Her small, firm and conical breasts stood out as white globes, starkly contrasted against the deep bronze of her Florida tan. In the centre of each, dark pink nipples created a further contrast, reminding Scheller of a pair of bull's-eye targets on a shooting range. He nodded with approval.

'Nice tits,' he muttered appreciatively. 'Small – but nice.' He paused for a moment, assessing the twin treasures with a more professional eye. 'What are you – thirty-four-B? You want I should make you a thirty-eight-C, maybe? That's my speciality, thirty-eight-C.'

Marylou nodded eagerly. 'And my nose,' she

reminded him. 'You said you could make my nose a little shorter.'

Scheller waved his hand in a vague gesture which seemed to signify agreement. 'Yeah, sure, babe, sure. Anything you want,' he muttered thickly. 'Be real nice to me and I might even throw in a little liposuction on that cute little fanny of yours.'

Marylou felt better at once, having re-established the terms of their strange contract. With breast augmentations costing up to forty thousand bucks, this little pick-up promised to pay the jackpot. She could only take him at his word, and hope, or at least dream. The same dream which had brought her from New York to work in the vacation paradise of the Florida Keys. Where a ghetto-born girl could find fun and excitement, mix with the rich, the powerful, the influential. Perhaps even be picked up and propositioned by the great Carl Scheller and offered free cosmetic surgery. Bullshit or a genuine offer, it was one hell of a chat-up line, that was for sure.

She fixed what she hoped was a sexy smile upon her lips. 'Sure I'll be nice to you, Mr Scheller. Real nice. Anything you want. You'd like me to be on top, maybe?'

Scheller shook his head. 'I'm too old for thrashing around in the sack like some fucking co-ed. That's how guys get heart attacks.' He zipped open his slacks, pulled them down to his knees and hooked out a half-hard penis from under the waistband of his boxer shorts, waggling it between his fingers. 'I want you to suck this,' he said flatly. 'Nothing fancy, no trying to jack me off at the same time hoping to make me come quickly. Just a nice, easy, slow blow job – plenty of lips and tongue and keep your mouth real wet and juicy.'

If Marylou was disappointed, she didn't show it. Her face was as blank as ever. In truth, she was quite relieved that Scheller didn't want anything kinky. Oral sex was fine, in fact she quite enjoyed the feel of a decent-sized cock throbbing between her lips. And she was good at it, which ought to make Scheller suitably grateful. Funny how older men always wanted blow jobs, she reflected, in a rare moment of philosophical thought. She moved to the side of the bed, dropping to her knees. At the end of the day, a cock was a cock, after all. Fucking or sucking – it was all fun.

Scheller had managed to coax his prick into full erection. Confident that it could now stand up on its own, he let it go. Grinning with anticipation, he made a pillow of his hands under the back of his head, propping himself up so he had a clear view of the girl's mouth moving towards the gently quivering shaft. Watching was half the enjoyment.

'Remember – nice and slow,' he reminded her as she licked her red lips and formed them into a soft ring. He exhaled in a faint moan of pleasure as Marylou pressed them against the glistening dome of his glans and sucked it into her mouth.

With the head firmly trapped between her lips, she fluttered her cheeks in and out, imagining that she was sucking on a lemon drop to encourage the flow of saliva. Rolling the spittle around in her mouth, she scooped it up with a curled tongue and spread it around the full circumference of the bulbous helmet. Then, still compressing her lips into a watertight seal, she slid downwards, bathing the first three or four inches of the stiff shaft in liquid warmth and holding her breath.

Scheller sighed, nodding his head in approval. 'That's nice,' he told her encouragingly. 'Now swallow it, give me some of that deep-throat stuff.'

Marylou did as she was told, pressing her head down until she had taken his entire length in her mouth and could feel the wiry coarseness of his pubic hair against her lips. The blunt tip of his cock was lodged against the back of her throat, threatening to choke her. She held it there as long as she could without gagging then slowly pushed it out with what air was left in her lungs, gulping in fresh air greedily.

'Again – only use your tongue this time,' Scheller urged, his voice trembling slightly with excitement.

Marylou swallowed his cock completely for a second time, more slowly now, allowing it to side over her tongue as she waggled it from side to side. Scheller lifted his hips from the bed, thrusting upwards in a futile attempt to plunge even deeper into her throat.

Marylou pulled back in an involuntary gesture, knowing that she could take no more. More in control of the situation once again, she pressed her tongue against the gently throbbing underside of his cock and ran it up and down with slow, lapping strokes.

Scheller groaned, squirming on the bunk. He raised his head, craning his neck forward, eager for a closer view of the girl's lush red lips clamped around the shaft of his cock. The sight excited him as much as the feel of her hot tongue against his quivering flesh. The muscles in his belly tightened, a delicious tingling rippling through his balls. He was close to coming, acutely aware that there was little time left to enjoy the full pleasures of Marylou's cunt-like mouth. His voice was an urgent hiss, spurring her on to greater efforts.

'Yeah, come on, baby. Show me how you really love it. Show me how much you really dig sucking cock.'

His prick was dancing in Marylou's mouth now as though she had swallowed a live frog, and knowing that it was almost over made her feel quite magnanimous. Indulging an old man's sexual fantasies seemed a small thing, and putting on a little show to keep him happy would cost her nothing. She played to his desires, rolling her big blue eyes with feigned rapture, sighing as though in the deepest throes of sexual passion.

She let his cock pop out of her mouth, eyeing it lovingly. Pursing her beautiful lips, she covered it with hot, wet kisses, then lapped it with her tongue like a cat enjoying a bowl of cream. Finally, sensing that he was about to pop, she sucked in a slow, deep breath and took the entire shaft into her mouth and throat for the last time.

Scheller came, not in one big gush but in a series of convulsive little spasms, each one spurting a thin stream of juice into the back of her throat. Marylou held his cock tightly in her mouth until the last tremor had faded away, then slid her lips back up the already wilting shaft. Tilting back her head, she swallowed the last of his come with a little purr of delight.

'You taste real good,' she told Scheller, giving him one last little thrill of pleasure.

The becalmed boat rocked, suddenly and violently, like it had been struck by the bow wave of a fast-moving, larger craft.

Marylou's eyes widened in alarm. 'What was that?'

Scheller shrugged carelessly. 'How the hell should I know?'

Nevertheless, he swung himself off the bunk, hitching up his pants. 'Maybe I'll just go up on deck and take a look.'

Marylou watched him disappear up the companionway steps. The small cabin echoed to the sounds of his footsteps across the deck for a few moments and then there was silence. It was a very long silence.

After nearly ten minutes, Marylou got worried. She called out his name a couple of times, but there was no answer. Finally, she went up on deck to see what was going on. The boat was deathly still again, stuck to the glass-like surface of the sea like a model. The deck was deserted.

Marylou's concern was taking on a keener edge now. Perhaps Scheller had gone overboard for a swim, she told herself, trying to fight a rising sense of panic. She moved to the stern rail, peering over it first to port and then to starboard across the unbroken waters. There was no sign of Scheller.

A sudden, sharp crack made her jump. Her eyes moved, automatically, towards the source of the sound, staring upwards to where the sail had abruptly billowed out, catching a wind which seemed to have sprung up from nowhere.

Marylou shivered, nervously biting her lower lip as she backed, slowly, towards the stern of the boat. The deck beneath her feet shuddered briefly as the twin Yamahas coughed into life again, as suddenly and mysteriously as they had cut out.

Marylou screamed.

TWO

HANNAH'S APARTMENT. AUGUST 2ND. 8.43 PM.

Naked, Hannah lay flat on his back, allowing Lauren to indulge herself in her favourite sexual position. Straddling him with her knees and firmly impaled upon his stiff cock, she ground the cheeks of her delicious ass between his thighs as she rocked herself towards orgasm.

Hannah sighed contentedly. 'You should have been a rodeo rider, you know that?' he murmured. 'You could have made a fortune on the mid-western circuit.'

Lauren giggled, redoubling her efforts to pump herself up and down the greasy pole of his cock. 'I do this for pleasure, not for profit.' She leaned forward, shaking her upper torso and making her lush cherry-nippled breasts sway enticingly in his face. 'Besides, there are fringe benefits.'

Mutual benefits, Hannah thought, taking up the tempting offer without hesitation. He wrapped his lips around the juicy ripeness of her left nipple, sucking and nibbling at it greedily.

And noisily. Above the mixed sounds of Hannah's contented sucking and Lauren's grunts of sexual exertion, neither of them heard the faint snick of a key in the lock or the soft passage of footsteps across the plush carpet.

Hannah was only aware of an intruder when Bonny Jarvis stood at the side of the bed, looking down on its busy occupants with an expression of faint disdain on her beautiful face. She lay a black briefcase down on the bedside table.

Completely unfazed, Hannah grinned up at her as he released Lauren's nipple from between his lips. 'Hi, Jarvis,' he said cheerily. 'How did you get in?'

Jarvis jiggled a small bunch of keys between finger and thumb. 'You gave me a pass key, remember? For emergencies.'

Hannah's face fell. 'This is an emergency?'

Jarvis shook her head. 'Not even a crisis. But it is official. I just couldn't be bothered to knock.'

Thrown off guard by the unexpected intrusion, Lauren tried to make the best of the situation. She sat up on her haunches, still impaled on Hannah's cock. 'Well, seeing how you're here, why don't you take your clothes off and join in? This boy's got enough for both of us. Believe me, I know.'

Jarvis flashed her a thin, condescending smile. 'That's his fantasy, not yours.' She returned her attention to Hannah, the smile fading. 'Well, can we get down to business?'

Party time was over, Hannah realised. He gave Lauren's gorgeous tits one last squeeze. 'You'd better go, sweetheart. I'll call you – OK?'

'Yeah, sure.' With obvious reluctance, the woman climbed off Hannah's still-erect cock and glared at Jarvis. 'I guess you get to finish this off, you lucky bitch.' She padded off across the bedroom to retrieve her clothes.

It was difficult not to be excited by Hannah's impressive hard-on, all slick and shiny from Lauren's internal juices, but Jarvis made a special effort. She ignored the prickling sensation between her thighs, forced her breathing rate down to a normal level. Her face was an impassive mask. 'I suggest you go and stick that under a cold shower,' she muttered icily.

'Yeah, good idea.' Hannah disappeared into the bathroom, emerging a few minutes later clad in a full-length robe. Lauren was just getting ready to leave.

Hannah escorted her to the door, kissed her on the cheek and patted her ass playfully. 'I really will call you,' he promised, pushing her out into the hallway. 'Could be a useful contact, that,' he told Jarvis, feeling the need to justify himself. 'Knows everything there is to know about old movies and movie stars. Works for the National Movie Archive.'

Jarvis was unimpressed. 'Where, the porno department?' she enquired sarcastically. She moved to the bedside table and snapped open the briefcase, pulling out a slim manilla file which she thrust towards him. 'Stone wants us to get on to this right away.'

Hannah opened the file. It contained a full-plate photo of a man in his late sixties and a single sheet of case notes. He studied them briefly, finally looking up at Jarvis with a confused frown. 'This is a simple missing persons case. So why us?'

Jarvis shook her head. 'Not just any missing person. Name's Carl Scheller. Retired now and living in Florida – but in his heyday he was one of the foremost plastic surgeons in the country. He operated on the wives of senators, congressmen – even top personnel within the Bureau itself.'

'And he's disappeared?'

Jarvis nodded. 'Without a trace. About two weeks ago.'

A mischievous grin spread across Hannah's face. 'Plastic surgeon – Florida. Perhaps he just melted in the sun,' he suggested.

The joke was not appreciated. Jarvis glared at him.

'Not funny, Hannah. There's something bizarre about this case. One minute he's on a boat fifty miles out to sea and the next he's just gone. And we have a witness who swears he didn't go over the side.'

Hannah shrugged. 'So it's a murder case. And the witness isn't a witness, she's a suspect.'

It was a reasonable hypothesis, Jarvis conceded with a slight nod. 'Ordinarily, I might agree with you. Only there's more. I spent some time going through old files before I came here. Just under a year ago, there was another disappearance – in the same area and under virtually identical circumstances. Only that time the victim was Walter Jerome – ex-NASA scientific advisor and generally thought to be one of the world's leading experts in cybernetics.'

Hannah digested this information carefully for a few seconds. 'OK, so it's a double mystery,' he admitted. 'But I still come back to my original question – why us?'

'Because both of these disappearances took place smack in the middle of the so-called Bermuda Triangle.' Jarvis paused, watching the sudden flicker of interest which lit up Hannah's eyes. 'I thought that might get you going,' she observed finally.

Hannah thought for a moment. 'What do we know about this guy Scheller so far?' he demanded.

'Not much. Except that he likes fucking young women. The younger the better.'

'Don't we all?' Hannah said, with a grin on his lips.

Only this time he wasn't joking.

THREE

KEY WEST, FLORIDA. AUGUST 4TH. 6.40 PM.

Hannah stowed the car in an underground car park at the intersection of Duval and Fleming and took the service elevator back up to street level. His first sight of Key West was an eye-opener, the entire island appearing to consist of little but wall-to-wall T-shirt shops, ice-cream parlours and gay bars. He reviewed the numerous pairs of homosexuals and gaudily dressed transvestites parading hand-in-hand with a mixture of distaste and disbelief.

'You mean Earnest Hemingway really *lived* here?' he asked Jarvis, who was waiting for him by the exit. 'The whole fucking place is crawling with faggots.'

Jarvis shrugged. 'Maybe it was a bit more butch in his time. These days, anything goes. Sex, drugs or a fast buck – they'll all interchangeable currency around here. The locals even made a half-assed attempt to succede from the Union in nineteen-eighty-two.'

'Wild town,' Hannah muttered, looking a bit more impressed as two busty young beach bimbos strolled by, wearing what looked like one very small bikini between them. 'Makes Miami look like Hicksville, Iowa.'

Jarvis sniffed. 'Yeah, well don't get carried away. We're here on business, remember?'

'How could I forget – with you here to remind me?' Hannah said sarcastically. Glancing around, his eyes picked out a small street-front bar, with tables out on the sidewalk. The clientele appeared to be mainly heterosexual. 'Could we at least grab a cold beer while we're figuring out our next move? This heat is killing me.'

Without waiting for an answer, he led the way to the nearest vacant table, sat down and ordered two ice-cold Budweisers.

Jarvis pulled a local street map from her purse, unfolded it and spread it out on the table, studying it carefully. 'Scheller had a beach-front condo down on Palm Avenue, only about four blocks from here. Seems to me our first priority is to talk to some of his neighbours, find out as much as we can about the guy.'

The waitress arrived with the beers. Hannah lifted one frosted bottle to his lips, taking a deep swig. 'And the girl who was with Scheller on the boat,' he pointed out. 'Someone ought to talk to her.'

Jarvis lifted one perfectly groomed eyebrow. 'Someone?'

Hannah grinned sheepishly. 'Well, doesn't make much sense the both of us covering the same territory. Share the workload, halve the time. You check on the neighbours, I'll interview the girl.'

She was being manipulated – and none too subtly, Jarvis realised. But ulterior motive or not, Hannah had a point. She fished Marylou's address from her purse, handing it to him across the table. 'Only, just for once, try to keep your dick in your pants, will you?'

Hannah finished his beer in a couple of gulps and rose to his feet, grinning. 'I always try,' he assured. 'What say we meet back here in a couple of hours.'

He was gone before Jarvis realised she'd also been shafted for the cheque.

★ ★ ★

Marylou's apartment was in the old town, in a white-painted, clapperboard-fronted three-storey building which had probably once been an old-style boarding house. Hannah checked the row of plain bell pushes at the top of the stoop. There were no security devices. He pushed open the front door and walked straight into the small lobby.

The girl lived on the second floor. Hannah climbed the stairs and knocked on the door. There was a rattle of bolts before it was opened on a safety chain and Marylou regarded him suspiciously through the crack.

'Marylou Vacarro?'

The girl nodded. 'So what's it to you?'

'Agent Hannah. I'd like to talk to you about the disappearance of Carl Scheller.'

Marylou looked flustered. 'Look, I've already talked to the cops and told them everything I know. The guy just vanished – like he'd been spirited away into thin air.'

Hannah delved in his shirt pocket and pulled out his Bureau ID card. 'I'm not a cop, Marylou. I work for the Federal Government. Can I come in?'

The girl hesitated for a moment, doubtful. Finally, she pushed the door shut, slipped the chain and opened it again.

'Thanks,' Hannah said, following her inside. He took in the apartment with a quick, practised and apparently casual glance. It was three-roomed, surprisingly spacious for a single tenant and, although it wasn't expensively furnished, it didn't look cheap.

He turned his attention to the girl. Jarvis had been right about Scheller liking them young, he thought. She was no more than nineteen, possibly younger, although nature had already put all the right curves in all the right places. It was difficult to tell under the make-up and the sexy image she projected. In daylight she looked merely pretty. At night, she would probably pass for beautiful. Jarvis's parting comment about keeping his dick in his pants flashed into his mind, and he was glad he hadn't actually promised.

Marylou had decided that Hannah didn't pose any immediate threat, relaxing slightly. 'You wanna beer?' she asked him.

Hannah nodded. 'That'd be nice.'

The girl crossed to the icebox, handing him a can he didn't recognise. Probably some cheap supermarket own brand, Hannah thought, opening it and raising it tentatively towards his lips. It was wet and cold. Other than that, it didn't have much going for it. Nevertheless, he smiled gratefully, to put her at ease.

'So, what do you want to know?' Marylou asked. 'Like I said to the cops, there ain't much I can tell you about Carl Scheller.'

'OK, so let's talk about you,' Hannah suggested. 'What do you do?'

The girl shrugged. 'Waitressing, a bit of bar work.'

'Pay good?' Hannah wanted to know.

Marylou's soft and kissable lips curled into a cynical sneer. 'What pay? It's tips only – but I get by.'

Hannah smiled thinly. 'From turning a few tricks on the side?'

The girl's eyes blazed. 'Listen, mister – I ain't no hooker.'

Hannah cast a slow, meaningful glance around the apartment. 'Pretty nice place to keep up on tips only,' he observed.

Marylou sighed resignedly. 'Alright, so I date a bit. A girl gets a few favours – know what I mean?'

Hannah nodded. 'Yeah, I know what you mean. That were Scheller came in?'

Marylou shook her head. 'No . . . well at least, not

really. It was the first time I'd been out with him. Some of the other girls told me about him – like being a famous cosmetic surgeon and all that. And how if he really liked a girl, he'd offer them free jobs, real expensive stuff.'

Nice angle, Hannah thought to himself. He was willing to bet that the Medical Licensing Board would just love to get hold of that one. To the girl, he said, 'I thought Scheller was retired?'

Marylou shrugged. 'Maybe he just liked to keep his hand in. But he still had a small clinic, right here on the Key. A regular nurse, too.'

Hannah's ears pricked at another possible lead. 'Nurse? Know her name, or where I can find her?'

Marylou disappointed him with another shake of her blonde head. 'Like I told you, it was my first date. We never got round to discussing details before he disappeared. But I guess you could ask around.'

'Yeah, I guess so.' Hannah sighed, figuring he wasn't going to get much else out of the girl. He glanced surreptitiously at his watch. The entire interview had taken less than fifteen minutes, and he'd told Jarvis two hours. Suddenly, he was in no hurry to leave.

'There's just one thing that puzzles me. Why a girl like you would be wanting plastic surgery anyway. You seem to have all the right bits in all the right places.'

The compliment had the desired effect. Marylou flushed with pride, momentarily, then giggled. She cupped her hands under her breasts, lifting them upwards and outwards. 'Scheller said he could give me an enhancement job. That was going to be his deal.'

Hannah licked his lips at the sight of the two pert little beauties straining against the thin cotton of the girl's blouse. 'I don't see why,' he murmured. 'They look pretty good to me. Anyway, you know what they say – anything more than a handful's a waste.'

Marylou giggled again. 'I guess you don't know much about this town, do you?' she asked. 'In my job, there's a nice simple rule – the bigger the tits, the bigger the tips.' She fell silent for a while, eyeing him thoughtfully. 'So you like what you see, huh?' she asked finally.

Hannah nodded emphatically. 'Sure.' There was a pitch coming, he was sure of it. He didn't have long to wait.

'I guess you Bureau guys have quite a bit of clout when it comes to the regular police, right?'

Hannah was guarded, not quite sure what was coming down. 'A bit,' he confirmed cautiously. 'Why?'

Marylou flashed him a sly smile. 'I guess you realise they've been hassling me, over this Scheller business. Maybe they think I pushed the poor bastard over the side or something, I dunno.'

'And did you?' Hannah asked bluntly.

'No way.' Marylou's denial was adamant. 'But I figure it's gonna take someone besides me to convince the pigs.'

It was almost out in the open now, but Hannah needed to tease a direct proposition out of the girl. 'So what are you suggesting?'

She looked him straight in the eyes. 'That maybe a word from you might get the bastards off my back.'

'And if it did?' Hannah asked. He wasn't going to commit himself.

Marylou smiled sexily. 'Then what I was telling you earlier – about a girl getting a few favours on this island,' she murmured. 'It works both ways – know what I mean?'

Just in case he didn't, she spelled it out for him. Hannah felt his cock twitch inside his pants as Marylou's fingers moved to the buttons of her blouse, popping them open. Momentarily, he thought of Jarvis, and the very faintest twinge of guilt flashed through his mind. It was gone before it really registered. He was thinking with his dick again, but it wasn't his fault. Could he help it if his pecker had a mind of its own?

Marylou had finished unbuttoning her blouse now, and was peeling the thin garment back off her smooth, sun-bronzed shoulders. She wore no brassiere, and Hannah could see she didn't need to. Flesh as firm and taut as that needed no artificial support. Hannah liked what he saw. Sure, they were a trifle smaller than his ideal, but any deficiency in size was more than compensated for by almost perfect shape and symmetry and the pert way they thrust upwards and outwards.

They were tits which practically begged to be squeezed, Hannah thought, a slight lump rising in his throat and an even bigger lump rising in his pants. He almost threw himself on the girl there and then, but the strip show wasn't over yet.

Marylou dropped her cotton shorts, stepping out of them and exposing what Hannah first took to be a pair of white panties. Then he realised that she wasn't wearing any, and that the light colour was merely untanned flesh which had been protected by a bikini bottom. The illusion had been heightened by the fact that her genital area was completely shaved, making the smooth mound of her pudenda particularly erotic.

With a name like Vacarro, she was probably of Hispanic descent, Hannah figured. That would make her natural hair colour dark, if not completely black. Shaving down under was probably the best way to get away with wearing suitably thin clothing for the Florida heat without flashing her pubes at everyone within six feet.

Regarding the girl in her full naked glory, Hannah could understand the appeal to a man like Scheller. Even to someone like himself, who liked their women a little more full-blown and mature, Marylou's sex appeal was devastating. The combination of youth, small breasts and that deliciously denuded mound of Venus created the archetypal sex kitten – the child/woman who radiated both innocence and pure lust at the same time. Hannah's erection was painful. There was a dull throbbing in his temples. He was beginning to sweat, despite the apartment's efficient air-conditioning system.

He stripped hurriedly. Completely naked, he glanced uncertainly at Marylou, feeling strangely embarrassed about the city pallor of his sun-starved body and waiting for the girl's next move. She had made all the running so far, and there was no point in changing a winning hand. He didn't have long to wait.

Marylou stepped towards him, reaching up to entwine her slim arms around the back of his neck. Her full lips parted, red and glistening, as she pulled his head down towards hers. Her mouth closed over his – soft, hot and smothering. Pressed tightly against him, her body seemed to melt like hot wax.

She withdrew from the clinch slowly. 'I like it best from behind,' she breathed huskily. 'But we can do it any way you want.'

Hannah didn't say anything. He was still a little breathless from the kiss. Taking his silence as assent, Marylou moved to an easy chair, bent over and placed her hands on the two arms. She spread her legs wide, arching her slim back so that the beautifully rounded cheeks of her ass reared up like a target.

Hannah gulped. Taking his twitching cock firmly in his hand, he moved into position behind her and guided the swollen head between the smooth cleft of her buttocks. One push, and he was gliding into her silky warmth with a shuddering groan of satisfaction.

Marylou's pussy was deliciously, impossibly tight. So

tight, in fact, that Hannah had to reach down and finger her asshole, just to check that he hadn't rammed into it by mistake. The innocently intended gesture provoked an unexpected reaction.

Marylou let out a little yelp, shaking her buttocks from side to side. 'Ooh, yes. Stick your finger up my ass. God, that really turns me on.'

It was a request that was easily satisfied. Hannah insinuated his finger into the tiny puckered crevice, screwing it gently through into her rectal passage.

Marylou screamed with pleasure, thrusting herself backwards on to Hannah's impaling cock. 'God, that's marvellous. Now wiggle it about. Fuck me and diddle me at the same time.'

Hannah did as he was told, stabbing his finger jerkily as he pumped his hips, thrusting deeper into the girl's glorious little honeypot. It took a few moments, but he finally had a nice concerted rhythm going with his cock gliding up and down the hot sleeve of her vulva and his finger gyrating smoothly in her ass.

Marylou moaned softly, her internal muscles clenching and unclenching with little spasms of pleasure. Hannah felt as though the shaft of his cock was being gripped by a velvet-gloved fist, jerking him off with loving care. His own sexual thrusting seemed quite superfluous, but he kept it up anyway, more out of instinct than need. He felt his balls slapping between her rounded buttocks, the liquid heat of her pre-orgasmic flow against the sensitive head of his prick.

Marylou's contractions were building up to a crescendo now, milking at his deeply buried shaft. Hannah knew he couldn't hold himself back for much longer, and he didn't want to. He threw his free hand up under the girl's belly, groping for one of her breasts.

His earlier comment had been spot-on. Anything more than a handful *was* a waste. Squeezing the firm flesh, he pulled himself against her body, driving his cock into her honeyed depths.

Marylou squealed with delight as he came, feeling his cock throb and pump inside her. She rolled her ass around in a last feverish burst of energy, desperate to reach her own climax before it softened.

Hannah's legs felt like jelly, the rest of his body awkward and uncoordinated. There wasn't much else he could do for the girl, and he felt guilty about it. Hoping it might help, he pumped his finger in and out of her anus like a piston.

Marylou's body stiffened and went rigid. She tilted her head back, her mouth falling slackly open and her eyes staring vacantly and unfocused at the ceiling. She began to make noises from somewhere deep in her throat – at first a low, moaning sound but it quickly rose in pitch and volume until it was a sustained, quavering wail. She came, moments later, with a series of convulsive shudders which made her body jump like a puppet with a broken string.

The tremors faded away and Marylou straightened up, pulling herself off Hannah's soft and exhausted prick. He removed his finger from her ass.

Marylou gave a long, contented sigh. 'That was great stuff,' she said, sounded like a woman of the world. She retrieved her clothes from the floor and got dressed. Suddenly, she was like a little girl again. 'You won't forget, will you?'

'Forget?' Hannah regarded her blankly.

'To persuade the cops to get off my case.'

'Oh no, right – I'll do what I can,' he muttered, falling in.

It seemed to satisfy the girl. She looked pleased with herself, as though she'd pulled off the business coup of the decade.

Standing there, naked, Hannah suddenly felt

exposed and rather foolish. He was wising up to the ways of Key West fast. He dressed as quickly as he could.

Marylou didn't speak again until he was at the door, about to let himself out. 'Oh, by the way – you don't know any decent plastic surgeons, do you?'

Hannah didn't answer, closing the door behind him.

FOUR

SCHELLER'S APARTMENT. 8.30 PM.

The condominium block which housed Scheller's apartment fronted directly on to a quarter-mile strip of private, chalk-white beach, fringed by twenty-foot palm trees. There was no public road access off the main drag of Palm Avenue, just a sweeping semicircular private drive in which Cadillacs, Lincolns and European sports coupés were much in evidence.

This was definitely the high-rent district, Jarvis thought. She doubted that a twenty-five-year lease on one of the condos would leave much change out of half a million bucks. Scheller had obviously retired in style.

The front entrance was protected by a single massive plate-glass door, fitted with a sophisticated electronic key-card security system. Inside the plush inner lobby, a uniformed rentacop sat in front of a bank of video monitors, a Smith & Wesson M38 snubnose revolver strapped meaningfully to his hip. The residents obviously got a lot of security for their money, Jarvis thought. She rapped on the door with the edge of her ID card to attract his attention, displaying it through the glass.

The guard eyed her with a surly glare as he overrode the electronic lock and let her in. The condominium block was his private little domain, of which he was the undisputed emperor. Interlopers were not welcome. 'What can I do for you, lady?'

'Carl Scheller's apartment,' Jarvis muttered curtly. 'I take it you've got a pass key?'

The man nodded grudgingly. 'Won't do you no good, though. The cops already went through the place with a fine toothcomb. They didn't find nuthin.'

Jarvis allowed herself a faint grin. 'Well they wouldn't, would they – being cops.' She took a certain perverse satisfaction from the guard's annoyance, who seemed to take the quip as a personal affront.

'Number eight, third floor,' he told her as he handed over the key. He glowered after her as she headed for the elevator.

The interior of the apartment was spotless, with everything neatly placed exactly where it should be. It was not a good sign. Obviously the whole place had been thoroughly and recently valeted by the cleaning staff, Jarvis reflected gloomily. Cops would never have left it so tidy after a search. It cut her chances of finding anything worthwhile to practically zero. Half-heartedly, set about giving the apartment a complete sweep.

The kitchen was empty. Even the icebox had been cleaned out and defrosted. The lounge was sparsely but expensively furnished and contained nothing of interest: a couch, a widescreen home-movie unit, a stereo console and a glass-topped coffee table bearing a month-old copy of *Scientific American*. There was also a liquor cabinet, but it was stocked only with glasses and a couple of bottles of club soda. The cops had probably taken anything alcoholic.

Jarvis moved to the bedroom, noting the king-sized waterbed and the video recording equipment carefully set up to film anything which took place on it. There was a tape rack next to the playback monitor, but it was empty. Something else the cops had taken for their private amusement. The walk-in closet, bearing racks of Armani lightweight suits and expensive silk shirts, told her that Scheller had been a snappy dresser, but little else. That left only the man's den, which was a cross between a study and a library.

The desk looked promising, Jarvis thought. It was also an easy target, the drawer locks already prised open, and none too expertly, by the KWPD. The top two furnished only a sheaf of personal papers – insurance policies, letters, receipts and a couple of unpaid utility bills. The deeper, bottom drawer held three box files, which Jarvis took out and opened.

Two of them contained Scheller's professional case files, some of them dating back to his Hollywood career in the early sixties. Jarvis waded through patient lists, times and dates of operations and dozens of 'before and after' photographs of nose jobs, breast augmentations and implants. Apart from discovering that the female population of Beverly Hills were probably carrying around seventy per cent of the world's available silicone resources in their chests, that the wife of a prominent Republican senator had once boasted a hooked nose and that one of the section chiefs in her own Bureau owed his reputation as a womaniser to a penis extension, Jarvis learned nothing.

The third box file was carefully labelled "Billy-Jo" and seemed to have been devoted to a single, very important patient for some reason. It was empty. Billy-Jo, whoever she was – or had been – was missing. Just like Scheller.

Disappointed, Jarvis replaced the files and closed the desk drawers. Her search had yielded absolutely nothing. With one last glance around the apartment, she let herself out into the hallway, turning to lock the door.

'Say, what's going on?' demanded a male voice behind her.

Jarvis jumped, whirling round to confront the man who had just stepped out of the elevator, carrying a big tub of ice cubes. His expression was openly suspicious for a few seconds, then, noting the key in her hand, it softened.

'Friend of Carl's, huh?'

Jarvis thought quickly. Since the man had made that assumption, it seemed a good idea to play along. He was obviously a neighbour, and knew Scheller. He might be more forthcoming with information on an informal, rather than an official, basis. She nodded silently.

The man's face broke into a suggestive leer. 'That figures,' he muttered, undressing her with his eyes. 'That guy sure knew how to pick his broads.'

Jarvis bristled instinctively at being referred to as a broad. Her milky-blue eyes frosted over. Misinterpreting the signs, the man's grin faded for a moment. 'Sorry to hear about Carl, by the way,' he muttered in half-hearted apology. 'He was a regular guy.'

That seemed to be it by way of mourning and eulogy. The man grinned again, tucking the ice bucket under his arm and extending his hand. 'Matt Fenton. I live in the next apartment, just down the hall.'

'Bonny Jarvis.' She accepted the proffered handshake and immediately wished she hadn't. It wasn't a handshake, it was a grope. Fenton's fingers were hot, their touch overly familiar as they insinuated themselves into her palm, stroking and pressing. It felt like he was fondling her already. 'Look, I got a little party going on down at my place,' Fenton said eagerly. 'If you were a friend of Carl's, it should be just your scene.'

It sounded ominous, Jarvis thought – but at least she'd get to meet some people who had known

Scheller. Perhaps one of them might offer some clue as to why the man should just disappear without trace. It wasn't much of a hope, but it was all she had. She fell into step behind Fenton, following him down the hall.

Fenton opened his apartment door, and Jarvis's worst fears were confirmed. The heady reek of raw alcohol and burning marijuana assaulted her nostrils immediately. Acapulco Gold, unless she was mistaken. And 'party' was a wild euphemism. What was going on was a full-blown orgy. Naked and semi-naked couples, trios and pretzel-like sexual formations of up to five individuals lay sprawled around the furniture and the lushly carpeted floor. There was probably music playing, but above the overall hubbub of grunts, mouthed obscenities and the slapping sounds of cocks in wet cunts and mouths, Jarvis couldn't hear it.

Her initial reaction was to back away, but Fenton pushed her through the door. 'Look, you'll have to excuse me for the moment,' he muttered. 'I got some unfinished business to attend to, but I'd like to get to you later. I'm not the jealous type, so you can fuck anyone you want in the meantime.' He paused, reaching up to slip one finger between her lips, stroking along the moist crease. 'You sure got a great mouth, though. You could save that for me.'

Jarvis resisted the impulse to bite the offending finger off at the second joint. It took a lot of effort.

With a parting, lascivious grin, Fenton left her. He paused at the bar just long enough to deposit the ice bucket, then headed for one of the bedrooms. Momentarily, through the open door, Jarvis saw the nature of his 'unfinished business'. On the bed, propped up against the thick pillows, a big-busted redhead lay with her legs splayed wide open, avidly plunging a large battery-powered vibrator in and out of her cunt as she waited for him to return.

Jarvis considered getting the hell out, but decided against it. She felt confident that she could more than handle Fenton if it came to a crunch, and most of the other guests were too busy enjoying themselves to bother her for the moment. She moved towards the bar herself – partly because she needed a stiff drink and partly because it happened to be the quietest place in the room.

She poured herself a healthy measure of Four Roses and perched herself on a stool, swivelling it around so she could observe the scene with cool, scientific detachment. As official custodian of the Sex Files, she could justify it as ongoing research. Besides, there was also a lot of coke sniffing and dealing going on, and knowing about it would give her some leverage if she needed it. In less than a minute, she had identified all the main sources of the drug and turned her attention to the sexual activity.

As orgies went, it was certainly lively, if not startlingly original. Just a flesh circus, a lot of people fucking each other in whatever fashion gave them the greatest pleasure.

In her direct line of vision, a young blonde was sprawled in a half-lying, half-seated position against the side of a chesterfield. Kneeling astride her, a fat, balding man jacked furiously at the shaft of his cock, dipping the great domed head in and out of her slackly open mouth. Apart from fingering her clitoris lazily, the girl was taking no active part in the proceedings. Probably stoned out of her brains, Jarvis thought, watching dispassionately as the man came, spraying pearly drops of spunk over the girl's face and neck. She seemed to come to life then, her eyes suddenly lighting up. She scooped the creamy jism up with the fingers of her free hand, transferring them to her mouth and licking them clean. The man rose to his feet, still holding his cock and looking around the room for something else to stick it into. He caught Jarvis's eyes upon him and swayed drunkenly towards her.

'Hey, you wanna suck this, sister?'

Jarvis pulled up the front of her blouse, just long enough and far enough to give him a clear view of the .38 automatic tucked down the front of her skirt. 'No – but do you want to suck this?' she countered.

The man gulped, his eyes popping. He lurched away, returning to the blonde and trying to stick his prick back between her lips. She had other ideas, her mouth already having been fed. She pulled him to the floor, rolled him over on to his back and started to climb on to his cock.

Jarvis turned her attention on a trio holding centre stage in the middle of the room, performing on the carpet. Naked and crouched on her hands and knees, a plump blonde joyfully dispensed multi-sexual pleasure from both ends. Kneeling behind her, and gripping her rounded buttocks with claw-like fingers, a musclebound refugee from *Baywatch* pumped his huge cock in and out of her tightly clenched ass with slow, ponderous strokes. Each forward thrust of his powerful thighs sent the blonde's face plunging deeper into the crotch of a raven-haired beauty seated in front of her. Her nose and mouth buried in the thick black bush of the woman's pussy, her tongue probed eagerly between the concealed fleshy lips to lap up the flowing juices.

Out of her corner of her eye, Jarvis saw the bedroom door open and Fenton's redhead emerged, with a mixture of sperm and love-juice dribbling down the inside of her thigh and a satisfied smile on her face. She walked into the lounge looking for the next piece of action, and wasn't long in finding it. She was soon locked in a passionate clinch with another impossibly good-looking beach-bum type, grinding her pelvis into his groin. They sank to the floor by mutual consent, locking themselves into a *soixante-neuf* configuration.

Moments later, Fenton himself stood naked in front of the open doorway, his eyes scanning the room. Lighting on Jarvis, he beckoned her over with a wave of his arm.

It was the chance she'd been waiting for, to isolate the man from the security of his friends and guests. She'd already decided on her tactics.

Fenton retreated to the bed as Jarvis walked in through the bedroom door. He still had a raging hard-on, she noticed – less than half a minute since he had finished with the redhead. Either the man had a permanent erection, or he was on something. Then a sweet, cloying odour reached her nostrils, and it all fell into place. The man was popping amyl nitrate capsules to keep his pecker up.

Fenton leered at her. 'Well, Bonny Jarvis. What's your little speciality, then? What are you gonna do for me?'

Jarvis kicked the bedroom door closed behind her with her heel. All pretence was over now. She fixed the man with a steely glare. 'Bust your fucking ass, if you don't answer some questions.' She pulled out her ID, brandishing it like a talisman. 'And it's *Agent* Jarvis, if you don't mind.'

Fenton's expression flashed through disappointment, surprise, and finally indignation. 'What the hell you talking about, lady? You got nothing on me.'

Jarvis raised a quizzical eyebrow. 'No? You got enough snow in this place to start a ski resort. I could bust you for dealing this second. How does three to five grab you?'

Despite the chill of the air conditioning, Fenton was sweating profusely. His thick neck was flushed and he seemed to be having some trouble breathing. His erection had already collapsed.

'What do you want to know?' he managed to croak.

'Scheller,' Jarvis snapped. 'I want everything you know about the man. For a start, who's Billy-Jo? What was she to Carl Scheller?'

Fenton's hand was clutching at his throat, as though he was trying to loosen a nonexistent necktie. His eyes bulged, starting to roll in their sockets.

She was no doctor, but Jarvis recognised the signs. Amyl nitrate was a dangerous stimulant at any time, but mixed with booze, sexual excess and God knew what else, it could be deadly. Having the frighteners put on him had probably tipped the balance. Fenton was having a heart attack.

Jarvis rushed to the bedside telephone and stabbed out 911. Reaching the paramedics, she dictated the address and replaced the receiver, hurrying over to Fenton's side.

His chest was heaving erratically as he fought to draw breath in short, sharp bursts. Even under the tan, his face looked grey. He wasn't going to make it, Jarvis thought, frustration welling up inside her.

She dropped to her knees at the side of the bed, pressing her lips to the man's ear. 'Billy-Jo,' she hissed urgently. 'What do you know about her?'

The ghost of a smile played about Fenton's ashen lips. They moved slowly, letting out faint words which Jarvis strained to catch.

'She was Carl's obsession,' Fenton managed to whisper. 'He always said he would have died for her.'

The man was fading now, his eyelids beginning to flutter.

'And did he?' Jarvis prompted, resisting a futile impulse to try and shake Fenton back to wakefulness.

There was no answer. The man's lips ceased moving, except for the faintest vibration as a shuddering and final breath was exhaled through them.

FIVE

POLICE HEADQUARTERS, KEY WEST. 9.10 PM.

Hannah flashed his Bureau ID card under the uniformed desk sergeant's nose. He didn't look too impressed, regarding both card and holder with an almost patronising amusement.

'So, what brings a big bad Federal man to Conch City?'

'I'm investigating the Carl Scheller disappearance,' Hannah told him. 'Who's the officer in charge?'

The sergeant jerked his head casually over his shoulder. 'Lieutenant Heller. Name's on the door.'

'Thanks.' Hannah strode towards a row of doors at the rear of the precinct. Heller's door was half open. A wave of hot, humid and cigar-enriched air greeted Hannah as he walked straight into the small office.

Heller sat under an open window, his chair propped back against the wall and his feet up on his desk. His florid face was shiny and beaded with sweat, the armpits of his light blue shirt damp and discoloured. His eyes, small and set wide apart, showed a momentary flash of interest as Hannah entered.

'Don't suppose you've come to fix the air conditioning?' he enquired hopefully. 'Goddamned thing's been on the fritz for three days now.'

Hannah shook his head apologetically. 'Sorry.' He

produced his ID again. 'Agent Hannah. I'm following up the disappearance of Carl Scheller.'

Heller swung his feet off the desk. He fished in the ashtray for the well-chewed stub of a small cheroot, stuck it between his plump lips and lit it. He plumed blue smoke at the ceiling before fixing his visitor with lidded, suspicious eyes. 'So what can I do for you, Hannah?'

Hannah shrugged. He still wasn't really sure what he was looking for. 'Anything you got on the guy, basically. Any record, for instance?'

Heller reached lazily for his computer keyboard, pulling it across the desk towards him. 'Let's take a look.' He punched in a command, waiting for the monitor to recall the relevant file. He scanned the display carefully for a few moments.

'Suspicion of statutory rape, January nineteen ninety-five. Held overnight and released. Case dropped after victim withdrew all charges. Our guess is he bought her off.'

'Anything else?' Hannah wanted to know.

'Possession of cocaine, May nineteen ninety-six. No charges brought.'

'No charges?' Hannah looked surprised.

Heller gave him an apologetic half-grin. 'Don't get too uptight, Federal man. Around here that's little more than a misdemeanour.'

'And that's it?' Hannah asked, disappointed.

Heller nodded. 'Looks like it. By local standards, your man was a model citizen.'

Hannah tried another tack. 'I understand Scheller was still practising cosmetic surgery. You got the address of his clinic?'

Heller shook his head. 'Afraid not.'

Hannah was getting irritated. 'Any way of finding out?'

Heller shrugged. 'You could try Yellow Pages. But if he wasn't licensed – and my guess is that he wasn't – then he won't be listed.'

Hannah's exasperation peaked. The whole laid-back attitude of the place was getting to him. Cops who didn't appear to care about their jobs, criminal charges that got dropped, unlicensed medical practices. 'For Chrissake, doesn't anyone bother about the rules round here?'

Heller's piggy little eyes narrowed. 'Listen, Hannah, there's a few things you gotta understand about the way things are around here. We got something like a sixty to seventy per cent transient population. Tourists, casual workers, snowbirds – even more than our fair share of illegals coming in through Cuba and Puerto Rico. It ain't that easy to keep track. There's maybe a thousand guys like Scheller – they come down here to retire and things don't quite work out how they'd planned. Maybe they ain't as well off as they thought, or they just get bored doing nothing all day. So they go back to work and keep it quiet so's the IRS can't catch up with them.'

'Nice speech, Heller,' Hannah said sourly. 'One of the best excuses for not doing your job I've heard all year.'

Heller glared at him. 'Will there be anything else, Mr Federal man?'

Hannah was about to turn on his heel and walk out. Almost as an afterthought, he remembered his promise to Marylou. 'Just one thing. The girl who was with Scheller when he disappeared, Marylou Vacarro. Is she still under suspicion?' Hannah asked. 'You think she pushed him?'

Heller sneered. 'That dumb broad? She couldn't push smack at a junkie's convention.'

'Then why are you guys still hassling her?' Hannah wanted to know.

Heller laughed outright. 'Because every cop we send around to her place gets laid,' he said candidly. 'They're standing in line to put their names down on the duty roster. Hell, Hannah – every job's gotta have its perks.'

'Well I want her left alone,' Hannah told him. 'She's my material witness now, and I want you guys off her back.'

Heller grinned knowingly. 'She fucked you too, huh?'

There really wasn't any answer to that one, and Hannah didn't try. He turned and walked out, with Heller's ribald laughter following him all the way to the exit.

Outside it was still hot and humid, but the air smelled a whole lot fresher. Hannah walked towards the bar where he'd arranged to meet Jarvis, turning things over in his head. Tracking down Scheller's nurse seemed to be the first priority. Some hunch told him that she held the key to the entire mystery.

Some of the things Marylou had said to him prickled in the back of his mind. 'Some of the other girls told me about him . . . how he'd offer them free jobs, real expensive stuff.' And another comment – made half jokingly, but probably deadly serious. 'The bigger the tits, the bigger the tips.'

Hannah had it all together by the time he reached the bar. Find one of Scheller's recent patients and she'd lead him straight to the clinic – and the nurse.

Jarvis was waiting for him. 'Get anything out of the girl?' she asked.

Hannah forced himself to keep a straight face. 'Not really. She doesn't know a thing. How about you?'

Jarvis shook her head. 'Maybe we'll have better luck tomorrow.' She glanced at her watch. It was 9.45 exactly. 'Well, I'm going to grab something to eat and go back to the hotel for an early night,' she announced. 'How about you?'

Hannah grinned at her. 'I'm going to find a young barmaid with big tits,' he said, not attempting any further explanation. He watched the look of contempt which flickered across his partner's face with a certain amount of satisfaction. Every now and again, he really enjoyed winding her up.

SIX

MASSACHUSETTS INSTITUTE OF TECHNOLOGY,
BOSTON. 10.06 PM.

It was the woman's scent, rather than her physical presence, which registered first. In a scientific laboratory where the reek of formaldehyde was the prevalent background odour, the smell of an expensive, musky French perfume was like an olfactory alarm bell.

Critchlow rose from his bench, abandoning the bacteriological cultures he had been studying. He turned to face his unexpected nocturnal visitor.

It was a hot summer night, yet the woman was wearing a full-length white mink coat, the collar pulled up to her ears. Oddly, this struck Critchlow as a bigger mystery than her sudden appearance. That, and the woman's face. He stared in utter disbelief at the huge blue eyes, the high, prominent cheekbones, the flawless complexion and the soft scarlet lips which seemed to be pursed into a permanent kiss. The entire vision of loveliness was framed in impeccably coiffured peroxide-blonde hair.

Critchlow blinked, unable to believe his eyes. Temporarily, he was completely stunned, unable to speak. 'Who are you?' he managed to croak finally.

The woman's sensuous lips parted in a smile, displaying two rows of gleaming white, perfectly capped teeth. 'You know who I am, Professor. I'm every adolescent masturbation fantasy you ever had. How many times did you jack off under the sheets, dreaming of me?'

It was true. He *did* know who she was. Just as he knew that she could not possibly exist. Not like this – not now. She was no fantasy, she was a nightmare. Critchlow shook his head, as if denial would make her disappear. Every scrap of logic in his scientific mind fought the evidence of his own eyes. 'No – it can't be,' he stammered.

The second part of the mystery floated to the surface of his brain. The lab door had been locked, he'd secured it himself over three hours previously. The laboratory itself was in the high-security wing of the campus, protected by one of the most sophisticated and technologically advanced systems ever devised. There were security guards on each of the underlying three levels of the building. It was impossible that the woman could have gained entrance to his laboratory – yet here she stood in front of him.

The fact that it *was* impossible brought fear for the first time. 'How did you get in? What do you want?' Critchlow muttered, through suddenly dry lips.

The woman's eyes sparkled. 'How I got here is not important,' she purred. 'What matters is that I am here. And what I want is you.'

She untied the belt of her coat, letting it hang free. Her fingers rose to her throat, unclipping the collar. The white mink fell open, revealing bare flesh. With a little wriggle, the woman shrugged it over her smooth shoulders and let it fall to the laboratory floor. Underneath, she was stark naked.

She was a goddess, a living statue. Critchlow's eyes widened as he took in the flawless beauty of her superb body. Her skin was creamy and unblemished, seeming to blend the sensuous vibrancy of living flesh with the opaque, smooth perfection of alabaster. Her breasts, full and heavy without being pendulous and tipped with the pinkest and most perfect nipples Critchlow had ever seen, could have been sculpted by a master craftsman. But her physical appeal was nothing to the raw sexual power which she seemed to carry like an aura, radiating outwards. If sex itself could be personified, Critchlow thought, then she was it.

He felt his gut tightening, a prickly heat building up between his thighs and rippling upwards into his crotch. His growing erection was tight inside his pants, already passing beyond mere discomfort into a physical ache.

The woman started to move towards him – slowly, and with all the sensuous grace of a catwalk model. As if hypnotised, Critchlow could only watch the faint jiggle of her breasts, the gentle undulation of her flaring hips.

She was upon him before he realised it, her hands reaching up to his shoulders, exerting gentle but irresistible downward pressure. Her scent filled his nostrils, making his blood race.

'I want your cock, Professor. I want you to fuck me,' she breathed, increasing the pressure on his shoulders.

Critchlow could not have resisted, even had he felt the need to do so. He sank slowly to his knees, rolled over on to his side and finally lay flat out on the laboratory floor.

The woman descended upon him, kneeling astride his thighs. With quick, deft fingers she unzipped his pants, teasing out his imprisoned cock until it stood free, erect and quivering. Her hand moved to the golden triangle in the valley of her thighs, her fingers prising open the fleshy lips of her labia and exposing the moist, glistening slit between them. Then, edging forwards, she settled her hot pussy mouth on the gleaming dome of his manhood and thrust herself down upon its full length.

Critchlow groaned in ecstasy. He wriggled his body briefly, as the moist warmth of her vagina enveloped his cock, sucking it in to a deep and cosseting tunnel of love. The sheer physical pleasure was like nothing he had ever known before. It was almost as if the blonde's cunt had been custom-made for his cock alone. All other thoughts fled from his mind. There was nothing else to do except just lie there, knowing that he was about to experience the sexual treat of his life. His eyes closed blissfully, as the woman began to rise and fall upon her knees in a smooth and forceful rhythm, fucking him with an intensity and passion he had only ever dreamed about.

SEVEN

SANDPIPER MOTEL, KEY WEST, FLORIDA. AUGUST 5TH. 12.54 AM.

The early night had gone by the board. Jarvis lay in bed, wide awake and poring over case notes on every missing persons case filed in Florida for the past three years. The bedside telephone rang. Jarvis dropped the files and reached out to pick up the receiver.

'Hello, Bonny.'

An instinctive shudder of revulsion rippled through her body as she recognised her caller. She'd know that wheezy, rasping voice anywhere.

'Lovelace, you slimeball. How the fuck did you get the number of this motel?'

A phlegmy, rattling parody of a laugh echoed over the line. It sounded like something nasty bubbling to the surface of a cesspit, Jarvis thought.

'I have my sources, Bonny – you know that. That's what makes me so useful to you.'

It wasn't a point which Jarvis wanted to argue. 'What do you want?' she demanded.

A self-pitying whine crept into the man's voice. It was obscene. 'Why, what I always want, Bonny. To help you. But of course, you'll have to do something for me in return.'

Jarvis felt like retching. Whatever Lovelace wanted, it

was bound to be unpleasant. It always was. But as an underground informant, he was in a league of his own, with access to leads which just couldn't be found through normal channels. Lovelace was the price she'd had to pay for cracking some of her most baffling cases.

Nevertheless, she played it cautiously. There was always the chance that the sadistic bastard was bullshitting, just to torment her. 'And what makes you think I need your help. Or even want it?'

There was a momentary silence. 'Carl Scheller,' Lovelace said finally. 'You're not getting very far with the case, are you?'

Jarvis didn't bother to ask him where he'd got his facts from. She had long since stopped wondering what gutters the low-life bastard crawled in to dig up information.

Her silence was answer enough for Lovelace. He had her hooked, and he knew it. 'What you need is a new lead,' he said smugly. 'And I can point you in the right direction.'

'And in return?'

Lovelace cackled again. 'I thought you might tell me a story,' he said.

Jarvis groaned under her breath. She wasn't in the mood for one of the man's twisted little games. 'What the hell are you talking about? What sort of story?'

Lovelace snickered. 'I guess you might call it a bedtime story.' He paused for a moment, breathing heavily. 'You wanna know what I'm doing right now, Bonny?'

She didn't, but she had a sinking feeling that she was about to find out anyway.

'I'm lying naked on top of my bed and I've got a hard-on that'd put a prize stallion to shame,' Lovelace told her. 'I've got my hand wrapped around my cock and I'm thinking about you. And now you're going to tell me how much you'd really love to be right here with me so I could ram it right up that cute little snatch of yours.' He paused for breath. 'In fact, you're going to tell me just how hot it makes you even thinking about it. How you'd like to lick my dick, wrap your lips around it. How you're so hungry for my cock you've got three fingers up your crack, frigging yourself like crazy. And I'm going to be jacking myself off all the time you're talking to me, Bonny. Now ain't that romantic?'

Jarvis's lips curled in disgust. She felt nauseous. 'You're one sick fuck, Lovelace. You know that?'

Again that crackling, phlegmy laugh. 'Atta girl, Bonny. You know how it turns me on when you talk dirty. Now, let's get down to it, shall we? Tell me about your cunt. Is it wet already?'

Jarvis fought back another wave of revulsion. Every instinct she had screamed for her to slam the telephone back in its cradle and go take a hot bath.

But she wouldn't, of course. The scum-bag was right – the Scheller case was showing every sign of being a dead end. And she'd done worse.

'Well?' Lovelace urged, taunting her. 'I'm waiting.'

Jarvis took a deep breath, fighting to keep the loathing out of her voice. 'Yeah, you're right, Lovelace,' she purred, trying to sound as though she meant it. 'Just thinking about that big beautiful cock of yours is making me drip like a sliced watermelon. I bet it's real stiff, hard as a bone.'

Lovelace let out a rasping sigh of contentment. 'Stiff and throbbing,' he assured her. 'And I'm rubbing it up and down real slow, to make the pleasure last. Now, you tell me about that juicy cunt of yours. How hot and slippery it feels as you slide your fingers in through your tight little crack.'

Jarvis allowed herself to slip into the game. The

mental image of Lovelace with one hand holding the telephone to his ear and the other curled around his dick was so pathetic and laughable that it helped her quell her disgust, if not keep it completely at bay.

'My pussy's so wet that I've got two fingers in already,' she lied.

'And your lips are all hot and wet too,' Lovelace prompted. 'You'd really love to feel my cock in your mouth. Your guts are aching, you're so hungry for it.'

He had one thing right, Jarvis told herself. Her guts were aching alright – but with revulsion, not lust.

'I'd want to lick it first,' she told him. 'I'd start at your balls, and work my way up slowly. Can you imagine the feel of my hot tongue gliding all the way up the shaft, reaching the top? Then, before I sucked it, I'd stick the point of my tongue into the slit, wiggling it around until you were begging me to take the whole head in my mouth and suck it like a lollipop.'

Lovelace groaned. Jarvis allowed herself a cynical grin, picturing the sick bastard twitching with frustration, jacking himself off like a steam-hammer. The sound of his erratic breathing hissed through the earpiece, giving her hope that the loathsome ordeal wouldn't last much longer.

'And then I'd start sucking it,' Jarvis went on. 'I'd take it right into my mouth and throat until I gagged, but I wouldn't let it stop. I'd fuck you with my mouth even if it choked me, using my tongue at the same time. Then you'd start to come, and I'd feel your beautiful cock throbbing between my lips as you pumped your hot sperm into my throat.'

Jarvis paused, wondering if she'd done enough. A relieved smile spread across her face as a drawn-out, wheezing sigh provided the answer. The line was silent for some time.

Slightly breathless, eventually Lovelace spoke. 'I've

just shot my load all over the sheets,' he informed her. 'If you were here, you'd want to lick it all up, wouldn't you?'

Now that it was practically over, Jarvis allowed herself the luxury of another little shudder. Typically, the bastard couldn't resist one last little humiliation. 'Of course, Lovelace. Every drop,' she assured him. 'Now, what about that lead?'

'The morning edition of the *Boston Sentinel*,' Lovelace said. 'Page five, column eight, fourth story down. Only a little snippet, but I think you'll find it interesting.'

It was less than Jarvis had hoped for. 'Is that it?' she queried irritably.

'That's it for now. I'll be in touch.'

It wasn't a prospect which Jarvis relished. 'Well don't be in too much of a hurry, will you?'

'Oh, believe me, Bonny – you'll be waiting for my next call with bated breath,' Lovelace muttered. His voice had taken on a gloating tone. 'You see, I said you'd find that little news story interesting – I didn't say you'd understand it. You'll need me to provide the connection – and it's going to take a bit more than one dirty phone call for that sort of information.'

The evil-minded sonofabitch had pulled one on her, Jarvis realised, too late. All her hate and loathing for the man came out in one explosive curse. 'You festering piece of dog shit,' she spat down the phone.

Lovelace shrugged off the insult with a throaty chuckle. The man had skin like a rhino. 'Like I said, Bonny – I'll be in touch. Good night – lover.'

He hung up.

EIGHT

EXTRACT FROM *BOSTON SENTINEL* 7.43 AM.

DEAD STAR SEDUCED ME, SAYS MIT BOFFIN

Claims by a top scientist that he was seduced by the ghost of late movie star Stella Devine were being dismissed by colleagues today as 'stress due to overwork'.

James Critchlow, 43, a professor of biochemistry at the prestigious Massachusetts Institute of Technology, made the bizarre claim last night, after security staff found him in his laboratory in a bemused state.

According to Professor Critchlow, the sixties' Hollywood superstar appeared late last night in his secure laboratory wearing nothing but a mink coat and forced him to have sex with her.

Faculty head, Wayne Proffit, told the *Sentinel*: 'We are currently investigating the theory that the possible leakage of an hallucinogenic drug could have caused such a fantasy. However, Professor Critchlow has been under a great deal of strain lately, due to pressures of work, and will be taking a four-week leave of absence on medical advice.'

Stella Devine, star of such Hollywood classics as *The Baron and the Blonde* died tragically in 1971, following an automobile accident. Although her badly burned body was identified by her ex-husband, controversy about her death has persisted to this day. Some people claim that Miss Devine faked her own death to escape the pressures of stardom, whilst others have hinted at a murder conspiracy, citing Miss Devine's romantic involvements with prominent political figures of the time.

NINE

SANDPIPER MOTEL, KEY WEST, FLORIDA. 9.04 AM.

Jarvis read the newspaper article she'd downloaded from the Internet for the fourth time, a thin smile on her lips. It didn't make much sense, and she couldn't quite figure out its full implication with the current case, but that bastard Lovelace had outsmarted himself – which gave her a great deal of satisfaction. At least she now knew who Billy-Jo was – or at least had been.

She dressed hurriedly, and headed for Hannah's room, six units along the corridor. She'd put her foot down about them taking adjoining hotel rooms early on in their working relationship, when she'd realised that Hannah rarely slept alone. Her cover story was that the sounds of his energetic and noisy humping kept her awake at night, but that was only a partial truth. In fact, close exposure to Hannah's love life made her incredibly horny, and she hated herself for it. She'd already lost count of the times she'd lain in bed fingering herself off to the sounds of grunts and squeaking bedsprings coming through the walls.

Hannah was awake, but still in bed – uncharacteristically alone. He sat up, propping himself against the pillows as Jarvis entered. He had a pretty impressive black eye, she noticed.

'Get in a fight?'

Hannah nodded. 'Sort of. I never figured you could get into so much trouble asking a woman if her tits were real or not.' He grinned ruefully. 'Still, it paid off in the end. I got the name and address of the nurse who worked with Scheller. Thought I'd go see her later today. How about you?'

Jarvis thrust the *Boston Sentinel* print-out under his nose. 'Read that.'

Hannah scanned it quickly, a dismissive grin forming on his face. 'Jeezus, Jarvis – this is garbage, silly season stuff. I get wet dreams about screwing Michelle Pfeiffer most nights of the week, but I don't make the newspapers.'

'It wasn't a dream.' Jarvis was deadly serious. 'And it wasn't a ghost either – unless you can capture a ghost on video. I made a phone call to MIT first thing this morning. What that newspaper article neglects to mention is that the all-night security monitors were running. They've got the whole thing on tape.'

Hannah still looked dubious. 'OK, but I still don't see the connection to Scheller.'

Jarvis shrugged. 'I'm not sure I do, either – but I'm assured that there *is* one.'

Hannah's eyes narrowed. 'Assured?'

'Confidential sources,' Jarvis said, with deliberate vagueness. She'd never told him about Lovelace and she never would. Having Hannah know her most intimate, loathsome secrets would be more than she could bear: how the perverted bastard would force her to commit the most depraved sexual acts in return for information; how once, in one of their first cases together, she had even sucked the man's oversized cock under a table in a sleazy nightclub, watched by a topless blonde hooker.

'So, what's the agenda?' Hannah asked, mercifully interrupting her thoughts.

She already had a schedule worked out. 'I'll take the air shuttle up to Miami and pick up a flight to Boston from there. I'll pick up the film, interview Critchlow if I can and fly back to Washington. You can join me when you've finished up down here.'

Hannah mulled it over for a while, finally nodding. 'Sounds good to me.' He grinned. 'In fact I can't wait to see how you react to a porno movie.'

Jarvis said nothing, some of the disgusting memories of Lovelace still lingering in her mind. She was aware that Hannah thought of her as a frigid, sexually uptight bitch. *Hannah, you don't know squat*, she thought to herself.

TEN

SCHELLER'S CLINIC, KEY WEST. 11.25 AM.

Lieutenant Heller had been right about the clinic being unlicensed. Without his unorthodox investigation methods, Hannah might never have found it. Situated above a Jewish delicatessen that sold chopped liver, it was a particularly bizarre location for a plastic surgeon to operate in.

Unregistered it might be, but there was nothing backstreet or sordid about the inside of the place. Hannah was impressed as he walked in. A scrupulously clean and tastefully decorated reception area gave way to a small waiting room playing soothing piped muzak. From there, a plain, closed door presumably led to the operating theatre, Hannah surmised.

The door opened as he hovered uncertainly in the reception area. The woman who came out, dressed in a crisply starched white nurse's uniform, was as impressive as the clinic itself.

Junoesque was the word which immediately sprang to Hannah's mind. The woman was tall – at least five nine – well proportioned and she carried herself with an elegant grace. She had a full, lush, but surprisingly firm-looking figure with prominent, high breasts and the legs of a dancer. She looked like a fitness freak, Hannah thought – the type who did regular work-outs every day and could turn sex into an aerobics session. He figured there probably wasn't a slack muscle in her entire body, and wondered how much of a contribution her employer had made to her general good looks.

The nurse's outfit was a bonus! Hannah liked uniforms.

She was probably in her early forties, he thought – one of his favourite vintages. The age when a woman was not only still eager, but also more than a little grateful. A winning combination.

'Valerie Mayfield? I'm Federal Agent Hannah. I'm investigating the disappearance of Carl Scheller. I wasn't sure if I'd find anybody here.'

The woman didn't look surprised. 'I thought someone would be round, sooner or later. I come in for a few hours every day – patient aftercare and that sort of thing. I like to keep things running, just in case . . .' Her voice tailed off for a moment. She regarded him sadly. 'You think Carl's dead?'

Hannah shrugged. 'We just don't know,' he admitted. 'I was hoping maybe you had some ideas on that score yourself. How close were you?'

Valerie raised a quizzical eyebrow. 'Apart from our working relationship, you mean? If you're asking did we have sex, the answer's no. At least not in recent years. A long time ago, but not anymore. His idea, not mine, by the way. Carl liked his stuff a lot younger – but I guess you already know that.'

Hannah didn't bother to confirm this. It seemed unnecessarily hurtful. 'Were you in love with him?' he asked sympathetically.

Valerie gave him a wry grin. 'Hell no. I just love sex – and Carl was good at it.' There was a meaningful pause, and Hannah got the distinct impression that she was making some sort of a point. 'How did you find me, anyway? The cops haven't got here yet.'

'A girl called Maxie, works in Macy's Bar,' Hannah told her.

Valerie thought for a moment, making the connection. 'Oh yeah, Carl fixed her up about a year ago. Terrific tits, huh? Carl was always a great tits man.'

Hannah fingered his swollen eye, ruefully. 'Pretty good left hook, too. She didn't get a muscle transplant at the same time, did she?'

Valerie seemed to notice the black eye for the first time, and was instantly nurse-like and solicitous. 'Hey, you want me to do something about that for you?'

She moved closer, apparently to inspect the damaged area. A lot closer than was strictly necessary, Hannah realised. He could feel the thrust of her full breasts against his chest, the heat of her nipples burning through the thin material of his shirt. Her breath was sweet and slightly minty in his nostrils. 'A little make-up – it'd hardly even notice anymore. And I'm sure we must have something around here to take that swelling down.'

She was no longer talking about his eye, Hannah thought. It wasn't the only part of him that was swollen now – and Valerie was pressed up against him close enough to notice. Just in case there was any room for doubt, she moved her body against his, picking up on her previous conversation.

'Yeah, when it came to tit jobs, Carl was a real artist.' She took a couple of steps back, thrusting out her own breasts for his inspection. 'You show me a man who can tell them from the real thing.'

Hannah couldn't, right at that moment. He gulped back a mouthful of saliva as Valerie's fingers moved to the top buttons of her uniform, picking them open and exposing her ample cleavage.

'Pretty good, huh?' Valerie demanded. It wasn't a question which needed a verbal answer. Hannah's bugged-out eyes did all the talking necessary.

She was still undoing buttons, the uniform now open almost to her waist. The two creamy mounds spilled out, bouncing gently up and down. Her eyes gleamed with pride. 'Now you tell me they don't look natural,' she challenged.

The twin treasures were perhaps a trifle *too* perfect in shape, their swelling softness tending towards the overblown, but Hannah didn't feel it was worth mentioning. He merely nodded with approval.

'You get some know-it-all smartasses who'll tell you they don't feel right but that's bullshit,' Valerie went on. 'You get the job done well and even a suckling baby couldn't tell the difference.' Her voice dropped to a husky purr as she pulled her shoulders back, thrusting her breasts forwards in offering. 'Go ahead, have a feel. See for yourself.'

She seemed to need reassurance, and Hannah was happy to provide it. He reached out, cupping his hands around each swelling globe. Valerie was right. They *did* feel just like the real thing. Warm, pliant, and yielding to the pressure of his fingers. Perhaps a shade on the firm side, but he wasn't quibbling. He ran his thumbs over the brown, wrinkled buttons of her areolae, testing their coral-tipped centres. His fingers strayed around the sides of each symmetrical hemisphere, sliding underneath their swollen weight.

Valerie chuckled softly. 'If you're feeling for lumpy bits, don't bother. I told you – Carl was an artist.'

He hadn't been – or not consciously, anyway. All the same, Hannah felt like a child caught at the cookie jar, and it stung him into conciliatory action. He caressed Valerie's magnificent tits more lovingly, as much for her pleasure as for his own. Taking each soft nipple between finger and thumb, he teased and twirled them until he felt them begin to harden.

Valerie let out a little gasp of delight. She moved in close against Hannah's body again, pressing her hot lips against his. Her tongue snaked into his mouth, sliding in and out in an openly suggestive gesture.

She pulled away finally. 'Come on,' she muttered, tugging at his arm. 'We'll use the operating table. It's not as good as a bed, but a lot better than doing it on the floor.'

Hannah followed her without protest. Right that minute, he'd have happily fucked her on a butcher's slab.

Stripped completely naked, Valerie's body wasn't quite as perfect as Hannah had imagined. There was a slight tendency to midriff bulge, and her hips were a bit too fleshy. Oddly, he found that these minor imperfections made her more appealing, not less – perhaps it was the reassurance that she was one hundred per cent woman, one hundred per cent real flesh.

She set the operating table at its minimum height and climbed on to it, holding out her arms to embrace him. 'Just don't be too gentle,' she warned him. 'I get frustrated as hell if I think a guy's holding himself back.'

It was something to take note of, Hannah thought. He climbed on top of her, slipping his hand between her already parted thighs. His fingers traced through the tangle of her pubic hair, seeking the moist heat of her slit. Her labial lips were already slightly open, pushed apart by the swollen protuberance of her unusually large clitoris. Two fingers slipped easily into the juicy passage, probing the fluid depths of her cunt.

Valerie groaned softly, lifting her buttocks from the table and pushing against his hand. 'I told you – don't be gentle,' she reminded him. 'Slam your fingers in as hard as you like. Ram your whole hand up if you want to.'

Hannah compromised with four bunched fingers, forcing them in right up to the second joint, jabbing them in and out like a thrusting prick.

'Oh, yeah!' Valerie gasped out her approval, shaking her ass from side to side. She began to play with her own tits, tweaking the erect nipples until they glowed cherry-red. With this added stimulation, she seemed quite content to lay there and be finger-fucked for a while, so Hannah paced himself accordingly. He had a pretty shrewd feeling that Valerie would turn out to be one wild fuck once things really got going, and he didn't fancy his chances of holding out for more than a couple of minutes. He continued to ream her wet cunt with his fingers, flipping his thumb back and forth against her clit.

Valerie was really getting worked up now, making a low-pitched humming noise in her throat. Her body convulsed upon the operating table as she thrust against Hannah's pumping fingers, urging him to push even deeper. Her pussy was oozing love-juice like a hot geyser, soaking his forearm. But his wrist was starting to tire now, matching the throbbing ache between his thighs.

Somehow, the urgency of his need communicated itself to Valerie. She reached down between their sweating bodies, grasping his hand and pulling it away from her cunt.

'Fuck me now, Hannah,' she breathed. 'I'm ready for your cock.'

Eagerly, gratefully, Hannah heaved himself into position as Valerie guided the blunt head of his prick towards the wet mouth of her pussy. He slid into her with a single thrust, gliding up the smooth and well-lubricated walls until he was buried in her up to the hilt. She let out a little scream, jerking up her knees and locking her arms around his neck.

'Yeah – go to it.'

Hannah needed no second bidding. He hadn't realised just how much his sexual tension had been building up while he diddled her with his fingers. Now, feeling the fluid heat of her pussy clamped around his prick, all his switches popped at once. His hips rose and fell in a blur as he let himself go, pumping into her with deep, savage strokes.

Valerie's nails raked his back, but Hannah hardly noticed the pain. He was fucking like a wild animal, oblivious to everything but his own desperate urges and the blind race towards orgasm. The woman's body vibrated beneath his, her knees slapping against his hips in perfect time with his pumping strokes. Her eyes were closed and her full lips parted in ecstasy.

They came together in a crashing wave as Hannah's cock jerked in a mighty, convulsive spasm and his swollen balls discharged their full load. Valerie's tight pussy contracted around him, holding his cock tight and sucking his hot come deep into her belly. Her legs flew up behind him, locking together in the small of his back and squeezing him like a vice. Her hips bucked frantically for a few more seconds, then her entire body seemed to melt.

Hannah lay on top of her for a long time, utterly exhausted. Finally, grunting with exertion, he mustered enough energy to clamber off, bracing himself against the side of the table for support. His limp, glistening dick was exactly at Valerie's eye level. She leaned forward, kissing it.

'You got another shot in there, or are you a strictly single-barrel man?' she murmured teasingly.

Hannah was still trying to catch his breath. 'Maybe later,' he told her. 'Right now I need a drink.'

Valerie swung her legs off the table, apparently still full of energy. She threw on her nurse's uniform.

'There's a coffee shop right across the street. I'll go get you a cup if you like.'

Hannah accepted the offer with a grateful nod. Having Valerie out of the way for a couple of minutes would give him the chance for a quick snoop around. He waited until she had closed the outer door behind her. Then, still naked, he padded through the waiting room into the reception area.

There was a large filing cabinet in one corner of the room. Hannah headed for it, relieved to find that Valerie had left it unlocked. He pulled out the top drawer and began flipping through its contents.

Valerie was right: Carl Scheller had been a great tits man. The first set of files were a breast fetishist's delight – hundreds of photographs of female frontal development in all possible shapes and sizes. Each picture was cross-coded with a reference number, but there were no names. Apart from being highly entertaining, the photo gallery was of little practical use. Somewhat reluctantly, Hannah closed the drawer and tried the second one down.

This time the contents looked more promising, consisting almost entirely of facial operations – a high proportion of which were highly and instantly recognisable. It was a real celebrity gallery, in fact – a distinguished record of Scheller's rich and famous clientele. Impressed, Hannah riffled through photographs of TV personalities, singers, movie stars. Then he came to one particular set of photographs which stopped him dead.

It was a face more highly recognisable than the others. A face which had passed beyond mere fame and into legend. Hannah whistled under his breath as he took in the trademark peroxide-blonde hair, the huge blue eyes, the high, prominent cheekbones and the soft scarlet lips pursed into a seemingly permanent kiss.

There was no mistaking the face of Stella Devine. Memories of the *Boston Sentinel* article and his earlier conversation with Jarvis crowded Hannah's mind – along with her strange conviction that there was a connection.

There were other photographs – profiles, whole body shots. Hannah was so engrossed in them that he failed to hear the door opening behind him. He started as Valerie stepped into the room, carrying two Styrofoam cups of hot coffee. He'd been caught at the cookie jar again.

She looked indignant at first, then merely disappointed. 'So it's back to business now, is it?' She handed him one of the cups.

Hannah took it, managing a sheepish, apologetic grin. ''Fraid so.' He displayed the sheaf of photos. 'Tell me about Stella Devine.'

Valerie crossed to the reception desk and sat down. She shrugged her shoulders. 'What's to tell? She was Carl's star patient, his personal Mona Lisa.'

'And that's all she was – just another patient?'

Valerie laughed. 'Hell, no. She was a bit more than that. Stella was the high point of his life, both personally and professionally. He *created* her, for Chrissake.'

'Created?' Hannah looked puzzled.

'I mean he practically built her, inch by inch, top to bottom. Nose, cheekbones, lips, tits, ass, thighs . . . you name it.' She paused, rising to her feet and crossing to the filing cabinet. She drew out another full-plate photo and returned, handing it to Hannah. 'Here, this'll show you what I mean.'

Hannah studied the picture carefully. It showed a plumpish, passably attractive teenager, with blue eyes and shoulder-length mousey-brown hair. Miss American small-town High School, circa 1955. Somebody's daughter.

Hannah frowned. 'This was Stella Devine?'

Valerie nodded. 'Or at least, it was an obscure little wannabee called Billy-Jo Eriksen. Usual story – small-town girl runs away from home, heads for California with dreams of making it in the movie business. There were thousands of 'em hanging round Hollywood in the fifties. Most of 'em ended up turning tricks or making pornos, but Billy-Jo got lucky. Carl was just getting started with a small practice in Los Angeles. He saw her picture in a third-rate pin-up magazine, thought she had potential. It took him two years, but he turned Billy-Jo into Stella Devine. Like they say, the rest is history. He made her career, and she made his reputation. Neither of them ever looked back.'

'They were lovers?' Hannah asked.

'Oh yeah, they were lovers alright. Of course, she dumped him as soon as she got famous, but he never forgot her. I guess that's why he spent the rest of his life screwing young girls. He was always trying to find another Billy-Jo.'

There was more than a trace of bitterness in the woman's tone, and Hannah couldn't help picking up on it. 'You seem to know a lot about it,' he pointed out, probing gently.

Valerie let out a short, cynical laugh. 'Well I would, wouldn't I? I was there at the time.' She was silent for a while, looking uncertain what to say next, or whether to speak at all. Finally, she made her mind up. She fixed Hannah with a cool, level gaze. 'Look, I lied to you earlier – when you asked me how close I was to Carl. I *was* in love with him, back then. But after Billy-Jo, it was never the same.'

It took some time for the full implications of this confession to sink into Hannah's brain. When it did, he gaped at the woman in disbelief. 'You were with Scheller back in those early years?'

Valerie sighed. 'Yeah, that makes me well over fifty, right? Fifty-six, as a matter of fact. Like I told you – Carl was the best there was.' A defiant, challenging grin spread across her face. 'Does that shock you? That a woman of my age should still be horny? To know that you've just screwed someone old enough to be your mother?'

Hannah shook his head in denial – and meant it. 'If it means anything at all, I think Carl Scheller was a fool, wasting his time with all that young stuff when he had you around.'

Valerie smiled gratefully. 'Thanks, Hannah – for being a true gentleman or a good liar. I'm not sure which.'

Hannah let it drop there. 'Do you know anything about Billy-Jo's background? Where she came from, why she ran away from home, for instance?'

Valerie shrugged. 'Some, not a lot. The story was that she left town to escape a scandal. She was supposedly the victim of a gang-rape, and a place like Woburn, Massachusetts just wasn't big enough to hide something like that.'

'Supposedly?' Hannah picked up on the word.

Valerie smiled thinly. 'Surely you must have heard all the rumours that Stella Devine was a raving nympho off screen? Well, they're true – believe me – and she was no girl scout even when she was Billy-Jo Eriksen. My guess is that the so-called rape was nothing more than a gangbang that got a little out of hand.' Her face clouded over. 'Look, are there going to be any more questions, or can we get down to that second shot you promised me? After all, you *are* already dressed for it.'

Hannah suddenly remembered he was still naked, and grinned sheepishly. 'Sure, but I need to make a call first. Mind if I use your phone?'

'Help yourself,' Valerie said generously. 'It won't

interfere with what I had in mind, anyway.' Even as Hannah reached for the telephone she was on her knees, nuzzling between his thighs.

He put in a collect call to Bureau headquarters in Washington, gave Section Chief Stone's security code and got straight through to his private office. By the time he was talking to the man himself, Valerie's hot lips were wrapped around his soft cock, sucking it back to life.

'Stone? It's Hannah. I'm just about finished down here in Florida and I'll be flying back tomorrow. Couple of things I need put in place in the meantime.'

Stone sounded surprised. 'Good to know you're still on the job, Hannah. I thought you'd have gone native by now, screwing yourself stupid with all those little beach bimbos.'

'Oh, sure.' Hannah's sarcasm was a double-bluff. 'Even as we speak I'm standing here bare-assed naked and there's a woman on the floor sucking my dick.'

'Very funny, Hannah,' Stone muttered wearily. 'Now, what do you want?'

'Every file you can pull on the dead movie actress Stella Devine,' Hannah told him. 'And anything the cops in Woburn, Massachusetts still have on a fifties' rape case involving a girl named Billy-Jo Eriksen.'

'I'll see what I can do,' Stone promised, and hung up.

Hannah dropped the receiver back in its cradle and concentrated on more immediate matters. Valerie had his balls in her hand, squeezing them gently as her soft lips fluted his cock. She sucked it into the back of her throat, rolled her tongue around it and blew it back out again. Letting it pop out of her mouth, she kissed it repeatedly before taking the swollen head between her lips once more.

Hannah had experienced a good few blow jobs in his

life, but he was impressed. Valerie's technique was flawless. Here was a woman who knew how to give great head.

Still, it was not really surprising, he philosophised to himself. After all, she had been around for a few years – more than enough time to get in a whole lot of practice.

ELEVEN

TRANSCRIPT OF DEAN CARTER INTERVIEW. WOBURN, MASSACHUSETTS PD. AUGUST 12TH 1957.
INTERROGATING OFFICERS O'BANYON AND ROLLINS.

O'BANYON: You're in big trouble, Dean. You know that, don't you? Rape is a serious charge.

DC: Look, it wasn't like that, Mr O'Banyon – honest! She's only saying it was rape 'cause her old man came out and caught us. Up to then it'd been all her idea.

ROLLINS: By "her", you're talking about Billy-Jo Eriksen – right?

DC: Of course.

O'BANYON: So what you're telling us is that Billy-Jo willingly agreed to have sex with you and three of your buddies?

DC: I'm telling you. She wasn't just willing, she suggested it in the first place.

ROLLINS: And you expect us to believe that?

DC: Listen, you just gotta talk to any of the guys at

High School, they'll tell you. Billy-Jo did stuff like that all the time. Hell, she'll put out for anybody. Around town they call her Billy-Jo Banger.

O'BANYON: Don't you be worrying, Dean. We'll be talking to your buddies alright. And you'd better all have the same story or you're all headed for the State Correction Center.

ROLLINS: So tell us in your own words exactly what happened. From the beginning.

DC: OK. Well, see, Chuck and Danny and me – we was just hanging out in the diner by the filling station—

ROLLINS: You're talking about Charles Mabin and Danny Rhodes?

DC: Yeah, right. So, like I say, we was just goofin' around, drinking coffee, eyeing up the chicks, when Al pulls up in his old man's new Chevvy soft-top and he's got Billy-Jo on the front seat.

O'BANYON: Al Jarret?

DC: Right. So we was all surprised, see? I mean, with all his old man's dough, Al can do a lot better than a pushover like Billy-Jo. And what with her family, and all. I mean, everybody knows her old man's a drunk and her mom cleans folks' houses . . .

O'BANYON: Cut the social crap, Dean, and get on with it.

DC: So while he was getting gas, we decided to go out and wind him up a bit, know what I mean?

ROLLINS: And whose idea was that?

DC: Oh, I dunno. Mine, I guess – but we all sorta came to it at the same time.

ROLLINS: Alright. So what happened next?

DC: Well, we all went out and started ribbing Al. Making cracks, you know. Like Chuck said, "Hope you like big red spots on your dick, Al, 'cause you'll have 'em in the morning." And then I made some joke about Billy-Jo having more dates than a five-year calendar . . . all that sorta stuff.

O'BANYON: And could Billy-Jo hear all this?

DC: Yeah. Well, I guess so. Didn't seem to bother her though.

O'BANYON: So what was her reaction?

DC: She just sits there grinning at us, y'know? And she's got this way of doing something with her lips – sorta pouting, like she's puckering up for a kiss, and it's a real turn-on, real sexy. Anyway, then she says, real loud, "If you guys had dicks as big as your mouths you might be some fuckin' use."

ROLLINS: Those were her exact words?

DC: Yeah. Billy-Jo can have a real dirty mouth on her sometimes. Anyway, this seems to upset Danny, who hasn't really said anything much up to now. He gets real mad, see, and starts hollerin' at Billy-Jo. "I got the biggest dick you never had, babe." And then he drops his hand to his zipper, like he's going to pull his pecker out right there in the gas station.

O'BANYON: So what's Al's reaction to all this, while you're all bad-mouthing his date?

DC: Well, he's been sorta good-natured about it up to now, but I guess he figured things were getting a little out of hand. That's when he runs over and puts his hand on Danny's chest.

O'BANYON: He struck him?

DC: No, it was more like a push – but we all thought there was gonna be a fight. And then Billy-Jo cuts in. Real cool, she says, "Why don't we settle this the easy way? Let's all drive somewhere quiet and find out who's got the biggest dick?"

ROLLINS: You're certain that Billy-Jo made that suggestion?

DC: Yeah, absolutely. And it really threw us, know what I mean? So, we all just looked at each other kinda dumbstruck for a few seconds. Then Al yells out, "Fuck it – I'm game if she is," and jumps into the driver's seat. Then Danny and Chuck and me piles in the back seat and we all drive up to Hudson's Point, just off the Interstate 95.

O'BANYON: OK. So you got there and parked. Then what happened?

DC: Well, I guess we were all sorta embarrassed for a while, you know. Like it'd all been a big joke when we jumped in the car, but things had cooled down while we were driving. But Billy-Jo, she wasn't going to let it drop. She jumps up on the front seat on her knees, looking down on us, and says: "Come on then you bunch of smartasses. Show me some meat." Then she peels off her sweater, and she ain't wearing no bra, and these beautiful big tits are just swinging there in front of our eyes. And when I say big, I really mean *big*. That Billy-Jo, she's built like a movie star or something – they're like a pair of melons . . .

O'BANYON: I think we get the picture, Dean. Just tell us what happened.

DC: Oh, yeah – right. So anyways, Billy-Jo's shaking her chest, just to make her tits jiggle a bit more. So these beauties are swinging about right in front of our eyes and she's giving us all this big sexy grin again. Then she says, "You can all feel 'em if you want to. I expect you bunch of Mamas' boys need all the help you can get to get a decent hard-on."

ROLLINS: Let's get this straight. You're claiming that Billy-Jo actually invited you to fondle her breasts?

DC: It's the truth, I swear it!

ROLLINS: OK. And did you?

DC: Well of course. I mean, no one's gonna turn down an invite like that, are they? We all had a good feel. Then Danny unzips himself and hauls out his dick right there on the back seat, and he's got this real boner on. "I'll show you what a real hard-on looks like," he tells Billy-Jo and then we all start laughing like crazy and we all got our peckers out as well.

O'BANYON: At this point had anyone suggested, or

made reference to the idea of having group intercourse with Billy-Jo?

DC: You mean a gangbang? Well, no, I guess we hadn't really thought about it up to then. I mean, we were all just sorta goofing around still. Only Billy-Jo, she ain't laughing at all. She's staring at our dicks and there's a real hungry look in her eyes. Her lips are all wet and shiny, and her tits are heaving like she's breathing funny. And then she suddenly tells us all to get out of the car and line up along the side.

ROLLINS: Which you did?

DC: Yeah, sure. Then Billy-Jo marches up and down the line, like she's making an inspection. And she grabs each of our dicks in turn, squeezing 'em real hard. Then she finally goes back to Chuck and grabs his cock again and says, "We got ourselves a winner." So Chuck asks her if he's the winner, what's his prize, and Billy-Jo says, "You get to screw me first."

O'BANYON: Now hold it right there, Dean. This is very important. Are you absolutely certain she used the word "first". She didn't just say, "You get to screw me."

DC: No, sir, Mr O'Banyon. She definitely said, "You get to screw me first."

O'BANYON: And from this, you implied that she was offering to have intercourse with each of you in turn?

DC: Well, yeah – but in fact it didn't really turn out that way.

ROLLINS: Hold it. Are you saying now that none of

you had sexual intercourse with Billy-Jo?

DC: No, sir. What I'm saying is that we didn't do it like you just said – in turn. We all sorta done it at once, if you know what I mean. All together.

O'BANYON: Jeezus Christ, this little creep's making me sick to my stomach. I gotta go outside and get some fresh air. You can finish this interview off – I've had it.

(BREAK IN TAPE FOR THREE MINUTES. RECORDING RESUMED AT 9.36 AM.)

ROLLINS: Alright, Dean. Let's start again. Now you said that all four of you had sex with Billy-Jo together. Are you now admitting that you subjected her to a mass rape attack?'

DC: Hell, no, sir. It wasn't like that at all. Like I told you right at the beginning, it was her idea.

ROLLINS: Explain.

DC: Well, Billy-Jo pulls off her skirt and panties and lays right down there on the grass by the side of the car. Then Chuck takes off his pants, and he's kneeling over her with his dick in his hand, just about to stick it in her, when she suddenly sits up. "I sure hate to think of you poor guys waiting around with your peckers hanging out," she says. "Why don't we save a bit of time?" Then she gives Chuck a push in the chest and knocks him over on to his back. Next thing, she's kneeling over him and stuffing his cock into her pussy. Then she sits down real hard on his dick and looks over at us guys. "I got one mouth and two hands," she tells us. "Take your pick."

ROLLINS: And what part did you play in what happened subsequently?

DC: Well, sir, I guess I was a bit slow off the mark. Danny got there first, and he just stuck his cock right in her face. Me and Al couldn't do anything else but just kneel down either side of Chuck so's Billy-Jo could reach our dicks. And she damn well did, too. She grabbed hold of Al's and my pecker and she started to jack us both off, real fast. Then she looked up at Danny, and pursed those thick red lips of hers into a big juicy "O" and let him stick it right into her mouth. Then she went real wild. She's bouncing herself up and down on Chuck's wanger, and she's sucking like crazy on Danny like he's got a lollipop instead of a prick, and she's pumping me and Al up and down for all she's worth. I don't mind telling you, I didn't last very long. Seeing Chuck's great big cock ramming in and out of her pussy, all wet with her juice – and watching Danny fuck her face . . . I was shootin' off my sauce pretty damn quick. In fact, I shot all over Danny's pants, and he was real pissed off about it.

ROLLINS: So you're telling me that you did not actually have sexual intercourse with Billy-Jo Eriksen?

DC: No, sir, I guess I rightly didn't – and I must be about the only guy in Woburn who ain't. Anyways, that's about it, for it was right about then that this beaten-up old Pontiac pulls up and Billy-Jo's old man jumps out. He's drunk as a skunk, and wild as hell. He hauls Billy-Jo off Chuck, and he starts screaming at her that she's a slut, and a whore, and a piece of white trash – and she's screaming back at him that we made her do it . . . and that's when we all made a run for the car, and got the hell outta there.

ROLLINS: Alright, Dean, that'll do for now. We'll want to talk to you again after we've interviewed your buddies.

RECORDING TERMINATED AT 9.42 AM.

TWELVE

BUREAU HEADQUARTERS, WASHINGTON, DC. AUGUST 6TH. 9.23 AM.

Hannah read the transcript of the Dean Carter interview, along with those of the other three youths, carefully and thoughtfully.

They were all virtually identical in content and as to the sequence of events which had taken place that night in 1957. Only the statement of Al Jarret differed slightly in that he described, gleefully and in graphic detail, how Billy-Jo had already sucked him off in the car prior to the meeting at the diner and the subsequent gangbang. 'Swallowing every drop,' he'd added, with relish.

Whether true or just a bit of bravado on Jarret's part, it seemed unimportant except to reinforce the fledgeling movie star's prodigious sexual appetite.

What Hannah found particularly telling was the actual timing of events. According to the Woburn Police Department log, Billy-Jo's father had made his accusation of rape at 11.47 pm on the night of August 11th. Dean Carter and Danny Rhodes had been picked up at 12.05 pm, Al Jarret and Chuck Mabin thirty minutes later. All four had been held overnight in separate cells pending their interrogations first thing the next morning. There had simply been no time or opportunity for the four young men to concoct and rehearse their story.

Therefore, Hannah concluded, it must be substantially true, confirming Valerie's claim that Stella Devine's nymphomaniac tendencies had been well established long before she got to Hollywood.

After that, there was all the confirmation in the world. The accompanying file, containing reports on Stella's known and rumoured sexual excesses, was a good three inches thick. The bulk of the material, consisting mainly of cuttings from scandal magazines, confidential film studio memos and biographical pieces written after her death, were of prurient interest only. There was another, more substantial document however, which drew Hannah's attention like a magnet. Compiled between 1967 and 1969, it was a highly detailed dossier on Stella's romantic and sexual affiliations with political figures of the day. Not only had she liked her men, it appeared, she'd liked them important. There was no indication of what agency or individual had commissioned the report, but there was something about the way in which the information had been assembled. Hannah smelled CIA. Strongly. Stella Devine had been under the security spotlight before.

Hannah finished up with the autopsy report. To the layman, it seemed perfectly efficient, official, and convincing. But the existence of the CIA file had already set up vague, niggling little doubts in his mind.

Could there have been a cover-up, some sort of conspiracy?

He shrugged it off, eventually. Paranoia was getting to be part of the job. He locked the files away in his desk and went in search of Jarvis. She should be back with the MIT security video by now.

THIRTEEN

PRIVATE VIEWING ROOM, BUREAU HQ. 10.07 AM.

'I thought we'd watch the film in here,' Jarvis explained. 'Rather than have half the guys in the department looking over our shoulders and making wise-ass cracks.'

Hannah flashed her a leery grin. 'Very cosy,' he muttered approvingly. 'Just you and me and a dirty movie.'

Jarvis ignored him. 'All the security cameras in the building were functioning perfectly,' she went on. 'So we've got shots from every angle, covering our mystery woman from the second she came in through the front entrance. I've had the technical boys make up a composite, so we can view it in a strict linear sequence.'

Hannah was impressed, but didn't bother to mention it. Jarvis operated her remote control, dimming the lights and starting the film running.

They both watched, fascinated, as a mink-coated figure stepped boldly up to the high-security door and touched the electronic key-card control box. The door swung open.

'That's the first part that nobody can figure out,' Jarvis said, voicing over. 'How she got that door to open. You'd need a pretty sophisticated electronic override system to crack that lock, and she doesn't appear to be carrying a device of any sort.'

They watched the woman progress across the lobby, towards the elevator. Jarvis thumbed a button, freeze-framing the film. 'Second mystery. See that security guard, caught just off camera? He appears to be looking straight in her direction, but he doesn't see her. Why?'

Hannah was unable to give her an answer. Jarvis set the video running again. The film jumped to the exterior door of Professor Critchlow's lab. The woman passed through with equal ease, the cameras now filming her from behind as she advanced towards Critchlow, who was still unaware of her presence.

He rose from his bench and turned, the camera capturing the look of shock and disbelief on his face.

The film jumped again, switching to another camera which caught the blonde from a three-quarters frontal angle. It faithfully recorded the mink slipping over her smooth and flawless shoulders and dropping to the floor. Just as Critchlow had, Hannah was able to appreciate the naked sexual appeal of the woman's lush body for the first time.

It was weird. He could be watching a rerun of an old Stella Devine movie, Hannah thought – except that she had never done a nude scene, and this was for real, not a movie. This realisation gave him a vicarious thrill, making his throat tighten and his cock twitch inside his pants. It was giving him strange vibes.

The blonde had forced Critchlow to the floor now, was unzipping him.

Hannah cast a half-sideways glance at Jarvis. 'For a professor, this guy's hung,' he observed jokily, seeking to ease the tension.

She didn't answer. Her face set impassively, her full lips compressed into a thin line, Jarvis was caught up in her own secret, intimate thoughts. She was watching one of her own deepest, innermost fantasies being played out – and she found it highly disturbing.

It was a recurring dream – forcing herself on an utterly strange man, making violent and passionate love to him; using his body – his cock – as a living dildo, bringing herself to the most spectacularly satisfying orgasm without the faintest trace of emotional contact. And afterwards, having used him, to simply walk away, leaving nothing of herself behind.

She didn't need an analyst to tell her the fantasy pointed to some deeply buried sexual hang-up. Nor did she want it dug up. Buried, she could live with it. Having it face the light of day scared the hell out of her.

Abruptly, she thrust the remote handset into Hannah's grasp. 'I've seen enough,' she muttered thickly. 'You can watch the rest on your own.'

Hannah stopped the video as he watched her leave, wondering what was going on in her head. It wasn't the first time. There was also a sense of relief. He'd been slightly embarrassed about his growing erection. He straightened his cock inside his pants, relieving some of the pressure, and settled back to watch the rest of the film.

Stella – Hannah had already subconsciously given the mystery blonde the dead actress's name – was kneeling over Critchlow's prostrate body now, her hand clasped firmly around the thick shaft of his swollen prick. Climbing on to it, she settled herself down until the beautiful rounded cheeks of her ass were pressed firmly between the man's thighs. Arching her back, her face raised towards the ceiling, she began to heave herself on and off his impaling manhood.

She built the movement up swiftly to a fast, furious rhythm – her smooth, luscious breasts swaying up and down in perfect time with her pumping buttocks. With a certain amount of reluctance, Hannah forced himself to look away from this enticing sight, concentrating on her face instead.

Stella's red lips were moist and glistening, parted slightly in what should have been an expression of sexual passion. Yet the rest of her face seemed strangely blank, her eyes fixed, unfocused and unblinking. It was almost as if she was in some kind of a trance, Hannah thought. Or maybe she was blindly following an established ritual; responding on a purely physical level to a pre-programmed mental urge.

Hannah's eyes dropped to her crotch again as it rose and fell upon Critchlow's cock, each upstroke revealing a quick pink flash of her stretched pussy lips. Reading her face again, the strangest thought came to him. Stella was fucking with her body for all it was worth – but not with her mind. It was as if the sexual act was an end in itself, a function of pure physical release rather than the pursuit of any pleasure. Perhaps it was just a manifestation of nymphomania in its purest form, Hannah told himself, lacking specific knowledge of the subject. He'd known a good few horny women in his time, but never a grade-A certifiable clinical case.

Critchlow's legs stiffened, the upper half of his body giving a convulsive shudder as he reached orgasm. What followed next looked strange, but happened so fast Hannah had to rewind the film. He played it through again in slow motion.

At the precise moment of Critchlow's ejaculation, Stella ceased pumping herself up and down on his prick abruptly, like a machine which had just been switched off. She reached down behind and under her own ass, grasping the man's balls in her hand and squeezing them. Then, just as she started to lift herself off his wilting cock, she gripped it at the base between finger and thumb and ran them all the way up to the tip. It reminded Hannah of someone squeezing out an empty tube of toothpaste – although in this case Stella seemed to want every last drop of his spunk inside her.

It was a coldly deliberate act, which didn't appear to give her any pleasure.

Hannah ran this final sequence through several more times without making any sense of it. Finally he fast-forwarded the video on to the point where Stella put her mink back on and then he switched off. He headed directly for Jarvis's office.

He eyed her quizzically as he walked in. 'Well, what do you think?'

Jarvis could only shrug. 'What the hell can I think? Stella Devine's been dead for over twenty-five years.'

'*Presumed* dead,' Hannah corrected. 'You heard all the stories. Stella, James Dean, Elvis Presley, Marco Delaney – they're twentieth-century myths.'

'Yeah – and Lee Harvey Oswald had an identical twin brother in the KGB. Come on, Hannah – let's be realistic. Even if Stella Devine had somehow faked her death – she was forty-two years old at the time of the car crash. She'd be using a goddamned Zimmer frame by now.'

Hannah was on the verge of telling her about Valerie, but decided to keep the more intimate details to himself. He compromised with the important part. 'Oh, by the way – I found out the connection, between Stella and Carl Scheller,' he said, sounding pleased with himself. 'She was his supreme creation. He virtually built her in plastic, from the body of an obscure little pin-up model called . . .'

'Billy-Jo Eriksen,' Jarvis interrupted, finishing the sentence for him.

'You knew?' Hannah sounded – and looked – disappointed.

'The Billy-Jo bit, anyhow.' Jarvis sucked at her teeth thoughtfully for a moment. 'Which brings me to about the only reasonably workable theory I've come up with so far. If we accept that the real Stella Devine is dead, then what we have here is a lookalike, a copy.'

It was Hannah's turn to interrupt. 'Why? Why should anyone want to turn themselves into a dead movie star?'

Jarvis shrugged. 'Ask a shrink, not me. People do weird things. Anyway, the point I'm making is that somebody had to carry out the surgical work. Scheller created Stella Devine once – why not a second time? My guess is that if we track down our Stella clone, we just might be one step closer to finding out why Scheller disappeared.'

Hannah wasn't convinced, but it was a theory he could go along with, at least. 'Alright – but I'd like to take that film to show Lauren tomorrow morning. That girlfriend of mine who works in the National Movie Archive, remember? They got equipment down there that can take a picture apart pixel by pixel then reassemble it any way you choose. If our Stella isn't the genuine article, she'll be able to show me the surgery scars.'

Jarvis didn't understand. 'So where will that get us?'

'I found the nurse who worked with Scheller for most of his career. If there *are* surgery scars, she ought to be able to recognise his handiwork.' Hannah paused, remembering the question he'd been meaning to ask her. 'Oh, by the way – did you get to speak with Professor Critchlow while you were in Boston?'

Jarvis shook her head. 'I drove down to his place in Woburn, but he'd gone away for a few days.'

Hannah did a double take. 'Did you say Woburn? That's where Billy-Jo Eriksen was born and raised. Now doesn't that strike you as bizarre?'

Jarvis thought about it for a moment, finally shaking her head. 'Coincidence maybe, not bizarre. It's a nice little suburb, just over twelve miles from Boston central and the MIT campus. Seems like just the sort of place a commuter like Critchlow would choose to live.'

Again, Hannah was unconvinced. 'Well I don't like coincidences,' he muttered heavily.

FOURTEEN

HANNAH'S APARTMENT. 11.25 PM.

Hannah reached for the light switch just inside the door as he let himself in, flipping it down. Nothing happened and he let out a mild cuss. He thought he could remember paying his last utility bill on time, but couldn't be sure. Perhaps it was just a blown bulb. Using the light from the hallway behind him, he set a course for the standard lamp in the far corner of the room.

He didn't make it. The door closed forcibly behind him, plunging the room into total darkness.

'Freeze, Hannah,' snapped a deep male voice behind him. 'Hands on head, feet eighteen inches apart . . . you know the drill.'

The man's tone was calm and authoritative, carrying an implied undertone of menace. Hannah did as he was told. He held his breath for several seconds. 'Can I turn round now?'

'If you want to. But don't try any heroics, Mr Hannah. Like going for that .38 you have tucked under your armpit.'

Hannah turned, slowly, straining his eyes. The man was just a dark shape near the doorway, his face completely shadowed. There was just enough light coming in through the drapes from the street outside to make out the gun in his hand, glinting with a dull, non-metallic sheen. An Austrian-made Glock 9mm automatic, Hannah concluded. They had no safety catch, allowing the user to get off an extremely rapid first shot. Fast, accurate and deadly. A professional's gun.

Oddly enough, this conclusion had a calming effect. Hannah relaxed slightly. If this had been a professional assassination, he'd be dead by now. Hit-men weren't known for time-wasting.

'Who the hell are you? What do you want with me?'

'Who I am's not important. What I want is your cooperation. And despite your reputation for insubordination, I expect to get it.'

Hannah was becoming bolder now, feeling his way towards more information. 'You seem to know a lot about me.'

'Oh, I do,' the man confirmed. 'Bureau Agent Thomas Hannah, security coding SFD eight seven nine six. Currently partnered with Agent Bonny Jarvis. Current case: Scheller, Carl.'

'Well that's one half of the social introductions bit disposed of,' Hannah muttered, with forced light-heartedness. 'So we're back to you. What do your friends call you?'

There was a mirthless chuckling sound. In the gloom, Hannah imagined he could see the man's face smiling and his stomach chilled again. Men who pointed guns and smiled were invariably the most ruthless – and the most dangerous!

'I don't have any friends, Mr Hannah. But I have been called Pepper – maybe because I can make things awful hot for people.'

Hannah nodded. 'Alright, Pepper – so what is it you want?'

Pepper was silent for a few moments. 'You pulled

security files on the late Stella Devine this morning,' he said finally, in a calm, matter-of-fact tone. 'The people I work for didn't like this. There's a lot of muck in those files which they'd rather not see stirred up again, if you take my meaning.'

Hannah was beginning to fall in. 'OK – so you're CIA or NSA. Which?'

'Let's just say we both work for the same country, Mr Hannah.' Pepper wasn't giving anything away. 'And it will be in both our interests if you immediately cease probing into things which don't concern you.'

'And if I refuse?'

Pepper sighed. 'That would be unfortunate. Let me put it this way – at the moment, you and your partner are working on an unexplained disappearance case. Within a week, the delightful Miss Jarvis could be working on another one – alone.' The man paused for effect. 'I do hope I make my point.'

The threat was chilling in its sincerity. Hannah nodded. 'Eloquently,' he muttered.

'Good. Then I'll say good night, Mr Hannah. I trust you sleep well. Now, turn your back to me again, if you don't mind. I know you're smart enough not to try and follow me.'

Pepper was reaching behind himself for the door handle as he spoke. As Hannah responded to his final request, he opened it and ducked out into the hallway.

Whirling round, Hannah caught just a brief glimpse of his departing back, and had to make do with that. Like Pepper had so rightly said – he was too smart to try and follow the man.

FIFTEEN

NATIONAL MOVIE ARCHIVE, WASHINGTON, DC.
AUGUST 7TH. 10.08 AM.

Lauren watched the film all the way through in total silence. Finally, when Stella had climbed off Critchlow's cock, she turned to face Hannah, her green eyes sparkling, her voice husky.

'Jesus Christ, Hannah. Where in hell did you get this piece of film? It's pure dynamite. I thought I knew just about everything there was to know about the movie business, and I'd have sworn on my life that Stella Devine never made a porno.'

'As far as I know, she didn't,' Hannah told her. 'That video was shot just a couple of days ago.'

Lauren looked puzzled. 'How could it have been? That was Stella in her prime. Sometime around the late sixties, at a guess.'

Hannah's face was serious. 'You mean you're convinced that really *was* Stella Devine?'

Lauren's bafflement was complete now. 'Well who the hell else could it have been?'

'A lookalike, maybe?' Hannah suggested.

Lauren shook her chestnut-brown curls. 'No way. I must have seen every one of her movies at least a hundred times. It's not just the looks. The way she moved, gestures, facial expressions . . . everything.'

'You're absolutely sure?'

'As sure as I can be. Look, if you want a double check, there's maybe something I can do with computer enhancement.' Without waiting for an answer, she ran the video back to where Stella was just starting to straddle Critchlow's prone form. Punching out keys on the console, she zoomed in for a blow-up.

'So how's a close-up of our professor's cock going to help us? Hannah asked, jokingly.

Lauren grinned. 'It might not do a lot for you, but it sure as hell pushes my buttons. That's quite a wanger your guy's got there.' She advanced the film in slow motion, stopping it again as Stella was just preparing to slip herself over the head of Critchlow's cock.

'During the filming of *The Renegade and the Runaway* there was an accident,' Lauren went on. 'There was a scene where Stella's character had to run across a battlefield to get to her wounded lover. Now either the special effects boys placed one of the explosive charges in the wrong place, or Stella was off track. Anyway, the charge went off right underneath her, and she took a piece of shrapnel in the inside of her left thigh. She wasn't badly hurt, but it left a small scar, shaped like a question mark.'

Hannah was impressed with the woman's knowledge. 'I never heard that,' he admitted.

Lauren smiled. 'Practically nobody outside the business ever did. The studio made Stella an ex-gratia payment of thirty-five thousand bucks and hushed it up, scared shitless their insurance company would blacklist them.' She moved the cursor a few centimetres to the right, framing off a small patch on Stella's thigh. Enhancing it again, she blew the frame up to full-screen size. 'There you go,' she announced triumphantly.

The small scar was clearly visible. Hannah had to

admit – it *did* look like a question mark. Someone trying to turn herself into a Stella lookalike would have had to go to a lot of unnecessary trouble to copy a detail like that. The implications were stunning. Temporarily, he was speechless.

Lauren took advantage of the break to return the film to Critchlow's cock in close-up. 'Mind if I run this bit through again? It gives me goose bumps.'

The computer was still set for slow motion. Jerkily, frame by frame, Stella's fleshy pink pussy lips edged down towards the swollen dome of Critchlow's huge cock. Then, suddenly, at the very last moment before genital contact, one of Stella's fingers flashed into view, stabbing deeply inside her cunt before withdrawing just as quickly.

'Strange. Wonder why the hell she did that?' Lauren murmured. She ran the film back, playing the same sequence through again at normal speed. This time, the movement was so quick it was just a blur. Hannah wasn't surprised that he had missed it on his earlier viewing.

'It looked almost as if she was reaching for something,' Lauren observed. 'Wonder what she expected to find up there?'

Hannah could only shrug, as puzzled as she was. 'Checking a diaphragm, maybe?' he suggested.

Lauren snorted, sounding dubious. 'If I was relying on a diaphragm for protection, I'd check it a damn sight more carefully than that.' She broke off suddenly, switching the film off and turning towards Hannah. There was a lascivious gleam in her eyes. 'But I'm not, as you well know. I'm on the pill, ready and willing, and we've got some unfinished business – remember? I seem to recall we had something pretty good going until that redhead bitch bust in on us.'

Hannah cast a nervous glance around the small

viewing room. 'Here? Right now?'

Lauren smiled. 'Relax. You told me this film was confidential so I booked the room for two hours and locked the doors. No one's going to disturb us. Besides, that film's made me feel hotter'n a hog in a heatwave.'

It wasn't exactly flattering to know that your girl has been turned on by another man's cock, Hannah thought – but it wasn't a situation he felt disposed to argue with. And Lauren was right – Jarvis *had* broken up a rather promising little number.

Not that his objection would have made any difference anyhow. Lauren had made her mind up, and she wasn't waiting for Hannah's permission. She leaned across and nuzzled into the crook of his neck, tickling his ear lobe with the tip of her tongue.

She was hot, sure enough, Hannah thought – but not so carried away that she'd forgotten his most erogenous zone. If she was trying to turn him on in the shortest possible time, she was going the right way about it. He shivered deliciously as her tongue progressed inside his ear, rolling wetly around its ridged contours. Her breath was hot and sweet against his neck, filling his mind with images of the pleasures to come.

He reached out, pressing his fingers against the swelling fullness of her left breast. The nipple was already swollen and erect, straining against the thin material of her blouse. Lauren let out a contented sigh as he rolled it with his fingertip, using his thumb to stroke the surrounding flesh.

She abandoned his ear, pressing her soft, hot lips against his. Her tongue slipped through, silently demanding the right of passage. Hannah opened his mouth slightly and a hot, wet snake uncoiled into his mouth, darting about like a wild thing.

She pulled away, finally, tearing off her blouse

without bothering to undo the buttons. She jumped to her feet, disposing of her skirt and panties with similar haste.

'I want to do it just like Stella did in the film,' she informed Hannah breathlessly. 'In fact, I want to do it *with* her.' Her fingers snaked towards the control console, pressing the "play" button. She dragged Hannah out into the aisle between the seats, urging him to lie down on his back where they both had a good view of the screen. Unzipping him and pulling out his tumescent prick, she quickly settled herself into the exact same position as her celluloid idol. Then, taking her cue from the action on the screen, she began to copy Stella Devine's every action.

It was a unique, mind-blowing experience, under which Hannah's senses reeled. On the flickering screen, Stella lowered herself on to the head of Critchlow's cock as Hannah felt the moist heat of Lauren's pussy engulf his. As Stella pumped herself up and down on Critchlow's stiff pole, so Lauren rose and fell upon his own. It was Virtual Reality gone mad, taken one step beyond technology. On the silent video screen, he could see the oversized figures miming out their passion whilst Lauren provided him with both the actual sensation and the sound effects. Lauren's grunts and gasps of pleasure could be coming from the lush lips of Stella Devine herself, and were the juicy smacking sounds of love-juice against stiff flesh coming from his cock or Critchlow's?

Hannah stopped struggling with the mental confusion and abandoned himself to simple sexual pleasure. It was only fair, he rationalised. If Lauren had been aroused by the sight of a screen prick, then why shouldn't he enjoy being fucked by Stella Devine?

With his eyes still on the screen, Hannah allowed his mind and body to fuse, melting together into the pure euphoria of sexual fantasy. He was living out the wet dreams of his youth as Stella thrust herself ever more deeply on to his cock, the hot, tight, slippery walls of her goddess-like cunt fluttering and pressing against his throbbing flesh.

It was Stella's beautiful breasts which quivered, so enticingly, above him. Hannah reached up, seizing the melon-like globes and fondling them with a sense of wonder, as though he had never caressed a pair of tits before.

His fantasy lover was deep in the throes of uninhibited sexual passion now, rising and falling upon his proud manhood with increasing fervour and desperation. The walls of her cunt vibrated against the shaft of his cock, the first tremors of an impending earthquake, and she was moaning loudly as her body passed into that strange hinterland between pain and pleasure.

The fantasy was fast approaching its climax. Like the last, bitter-sweet moments between sleep and awakening, it suddenly seemed more lucid, more intense. Hannah threw his mind and body into it with a sense of desperation, vaguely aware that he would never quite recapture such ecstatic pleasure again.

The fluid gush of Stella's orgasm bathed his cock in liquid heat. Hannah heaved his buttocks from the floor, his stomach muscles tensed against her body weight. He thrust upwards with frenzied strokes, grunting heavily with both exertion and pain as his pelvis smashed against hers.

Finally, with a roar of triumph, Hannah did what ten million other men had lusted to do over nearly three decades. With a rapturous, convulsive shudder, he emptied his cock and balls into one of the greatest sex symbols of all time.

SIXTEEN

BUREAU HQ, WASHINGTON, DC. 12.14 PM.

Jarvis's office was empty, her black briefcase missing from its usual place on her desk. Leaving the room, Hannah crossed to the secretarial pool across the hall. 'Anybody seen Jarvis?'

One of the girls rose from her desk, brandishing a buff-coloured envelope. 'She's flown across to LA for a couple of days. She left you a letter.'

Hannah took the envelope, the twin emotions of disappointment and concern melding into a single feeling of frustration. Disappointment because he'd wanted to tell her the incredible news about Stella Devine, and concern because he'd planned to warn her about Pepper's threat.

He carried the envelope to his own office, sat down and opened it. It contained a short, handwritten note, and two newspaper cuttings. He read the note first.

'Hannah, looks like our Stella clone has been a busy girl in the last twenty-four hours. Two more seductions, obviously worth following up. Only this time I've taken the interesting one for myself.'

Hannah didn't quite understand the last sentence. At least, not until he picked up the first cutting, taken from the *National Enquirer*, and read it through.

IS WARREN GOING WACKO?

Warren Eastleigh, heart-throb star of the box-office blockbuster *Easy Kill* and currently one of Tinseltown's hottest properties, could be on the verge of a nervous breakdown, according to confidential sources here in Hollywood.

Warren, already becoming something of a modern legend for his wild lifestyle and unashamed publicity-seeking, has shocked friends and colleagues by claiming that he is having an affair with the reincarnation of sixties' screen siren Stella Devine. The star's unconventional beliefs and interest in occult phenomena are already well documented, but this is the first time he has claimed personal experience.

Actress Michelle Devereau, strongly tipped to star opposite Warren in the forthcoming remake of *The Love Triangle*, is quoted as saying: "The guy has got to be sick in the head, trying on a publicity stunt like that."

Warren made his bizarre claim at a studio party held to celebrate the end of filming on *Easy Kill 2*. Other guests at the party told *The Enquirer* that he was "reasonably sober" by his own hell-raising standards, and apparently quite serious.

Studio boss Cedric Jefferson commented: "In my opinion, the guy needs to sack either his publicity agent or his analyst – possibly both."

Hannah turned his attention to the second cutting, from the *Wyoming Daily Star*. It contained an even briefer report that a woman fitting Stella Devine's description had been seen leaving the contestants' changing rooms at the Cheyenne Annual Rodeo. A wry grin formed on his face as he finished the clipping. Judging from Stella's performance with Professor Critchlow, her second choice seemed particularly apt.

The grin faded as he cast a brief glance back at Jarvis's note, realising that she expected him to fly out to the mid-west to check it out.

She hadn't been kidding when she said she'd taken the interesting one for herself!

SEVENTEEN

BELAIR, LOS ANGELES, CALIFORNIA. AUGUST 8TH.
11.26 AM.

Eastleigh's mansion was comparatively modest by Hollywood standards – merely a twelve-roomed property set in some three and a half acres of landscaped gardens and guarded by an eight-foot perimeter wall. The two goons acting as minders on the outer gates looked like they'd be happier working for a Mafia boss than for a movie star, but they backed off once Jarvis showed them her ID.

She cruised up the drive in her rented Chrysler Lebaron, parking in one of the six laid-out bays. A maid answered the door, showing her into a huge conservatory and day room overlooking the outdoor pool. Seating herself in a suspended basket chair, Jarvis waited for the man twice voted "The Most Handsome Hunk of Hollywood" to make his grand entrance.

She was pleasantly surprised. Warren Eastleigh walked, rather than swept into the room. It was nearly noon, but he was wearing a Japanese silk robe, suggesting that he'd come straight from his bed, yet he was perfectly groomed. He looked and acted relaxed and perfectly natural. There was none of the posturing or swagger which Jarvis had expected. He could have been any regular guy straight off the street – except for his heart-stopping good looks and the sheer charisma which seemed to emanate from him in flowing, powerful waves. In short, he had what is often referred to as "star quality", but there was more to it than that.

On screen, Eastleigh displayed a macho, aggressive sexuality which appealed directly to the more submissive side of the female psyche. In the flesh, this raw sexual appeal was just as strong, but it was tempered with a quiet confidence which increased, rather than decreased, the effect. There was also a boyish innocence about the man, as though he was unaware of his own power, which Jarvis found particularly appealing.

She found his overall presence quite devastating, and the strength of her own reaction unsettling. She felt like a child on her first trip to Disneyland, completely overawed by the larger-than-life magic of it all.

But the undercurrents of her thoughts were a lot less innocent. There weren't many men who could bust through her carefully erected defences and appeal directly to her own smouldering sexuality – but Warren Eastleigh was one of them. She found herself wondering if he was totally naked underneath the robe, even speculating on the size and shape of his sexual equipment. He would have a cock designed for performance, not display, she fantasised. Probably no more than two or three inches above average in length, but particularly thick, and heavily veined. A good, strong, satisfying cock – quick to rise and slow to fall. She suddenly felt the overpowering urge to thrust her hand through the opening of his robe and find out for sure.

Eastleigh's thick, sensual lips curved into a friendly, almost apologetic smile, revealing a perfect set of pearly-white teeth. 'Look, I'm sorry, but I'm not giving any interviews just now.'

Jarvis made a mental effort to control her wildly erotic thoughts. She pulled her ID and showed it to him, uncomfortably aware that her palms and fingertips were sweating. 'This isn't an interview.'

'Oh.' Eastleigh looked puzzled, but not unduly concerned. 'So what have I done to upset the Federal Government?'

'Just a routine enquiry,' Jarvis said, giving him the standard spiel. 'We were rather interested in your story about Stella Devine.'

She had expected embarrassment, and was surprised when it wasn't apparent. The man faced her squarely, his features open and sincere. His smile was thin, perhaps guarded, but certainly not sheepish. When he spoke, his tone was without guile. 'Most people assumed that was just a publicity stunt. Or that I was starting to crack up. You don't, obviously. Why?'

Jarvis answered him with equal directness. 'Because you're not the only one. Someone looking like Stella Devine has appeared to at least two other people.'

Eastleigh was silent for a few moments, his forehead creased in contemplative thought. 'Then I was right,' he murmured eventually. 'She *is* back for a purpose.'

Jarvis gaped at him. 'Are you telling me that you really believe Stella Devine has been reincarnated?'

Eastleigh nodded. Again, the sincerity on his face was absolute. 'Oh yes,' he said calmly. 'No doubt about it. She was here, with me. We made love.' He broke off to point out through the sliding glass doors of the conservatory. 'Right out there, as a matter of fact. By the side of the pool.'

It was already tempting to dismiss the guy as a flake, but Jarvis couldn't quite bring herself to do that. There was also a strange part of her which wanted, even needed, to believe him.

'You said "a purpose". What did you mean by that?'

Eastleigh smiled again – this time with the knowing,

confident air of the true believer. 'A lot of people think that everyone is reincarnated – that all souls are reborn into a new body – but it's not like that at all.'

Jarvis raised one eyebrow. 'It's not?'

Eastleigh shook his head. 'Oh no, far from it. Memories, talents, even facets of the personalities of dead people are often assimilated back into the living, of course – but only the most forceful and powerful of souls are capable of making the journey back in a complete physical form. Even then, they have to be driven by some really strong motivation. They need a purpose, if you like.'

'Such as?'

'It could be a lot of things. To put right some wrong which was done to them in their previous lives, for instance. Or sometimes because bits of themselves have accidentally been transferred into an unsuitable, or undeserving host. In those sort of cases, they might simply want to retrieve the part which doesn't fit, or perhaps teach the new host how to bring it out, make the most of it.'

He fell silent for a long time, fixing Jarvis with the quiet confidence she found so unnerving. 'There's part of Stella in you, did you know that?' he told her eventually.

Jarvis laughed nervously – mainly because she couldn't think of another response. 'Really? Which part?'

'The sexual part,' Eastleigh answered candidly. 'You're a very beautiful and very sensual woman – yet you struggle to conceal it, to deny yourself pleasure. Now why is that, do you suppose?'

The words hit Jarvis with the effect of a physical blow. The man seemed to be able to reach inside her, twist parts of her that hadn't been touched in years. Instinctively, she wanted to recoil, draw in upon herself

– but some deeper, inner voice screamed out for her to respond.

'Because it makes me vulnerable,' she said, in little more than whisper. 'It makes me aware of my own weakness, and I can't afford that luxury.'

Eastleigh smiled. 'Would you like to make love to me? I'd certainly like to make love to you.'

The pin entered the balloon, popping it inside Jarvis's head. Physically, she felt as though the bond which had seemed to stretch between her and Warren Eastleigh had suddenly snapped back like a broken elastic band, stinging her flesh.

Her milky-blue eyes were suddenly cold, her lips already peeling back in a gesture of contempt. 'I did – until you just blew it,' she said bitterly. 'You just proved that you're the very kind of arrogant sexual opportunist I have to protect myself against.'

Eastleigh was instantly contrite. 'I'm sorry. You've misunderstood,' he murmured. He reached out, taking Jarvis's hand. 'Look, bear with me for a while, please? I'd like to show you something.'

Despite her anger, Jarvis let him lead her across the day room to a small table. On it stood a videophone and an address book.

'Terrific little gadgets, these,' Eastleigh said, indicating the phone. 'Let you know exactly who you're talking to.' He picked up the book and thrust it into Jarvis's hand. 'Choose a number – any one you like.'

The part of her which was still mesmerised by the man's incredible presence obeyed automatically. Jarvis opened the book, which read like a Hollywood *Who's Who* of female stars and starlets. The name Helen Etheridge leapt off the page at her. The undisputed sex goddess of the moment, she was the nineties' equivalent of what Stella Devine had been in her own day.

Jarvis stabbed her finger down on the actress's telephone number.

Eastleigh nodded, smiling. 'Good choice.' He picked up the videophone, punching out the number.

The machine flickered into life. Helen Etheridge's face came up on the small screen. Even without full screen make-up, she still looked gorgeous. The lips that a million men dreamed of kissing curled into a smile as she recognised her caller.

'Hi, Warren. What can I do for you?'

Eastleigh didn't mince words. 'Hi, Helen. Hey, listen, honey – you wanna come over to my place and fuck sometime?'

The actress giggled. 'Anytime, Warren, you know that. You want I should come over right now? I can be there in fifteen minutes.'

Eastleigh shook his head. 'No, I'm busy right now, babe. How about sometime tomorrow?'

'It's a date.' She rang off, blanking the screen.

Eastleigh hung up the phone, turning to Jarvis, who regarded him frostily. 'Am I supposed to be impressed?'

'Just trying to make a point, that's all.' Just in case it wasn't clear, he spelled it out. 'Look, I can have just about any woman in Hollywood I want, anytime I want her. Only right now I really want to make love to you. Doesn't that mean something to you?'

Jarvis felt herself beginning to melt. There was a sensation of warmth spreading all the way down from her neck to her toes. Her nipples were tingling and she felt breathless. The dryness in her throat lent a husky tone to her voice. 'Yeah, I guess it does.'

'Good.' Eastleigh took her hand again. 'Just relax,' he told her as he led her towards the master bedroom. 'Just let that Stella part of you come out naturally.'

★ ★ ★

Eastleigh whistled appreciatively as Jarvis finally discarded her panties and stood in all her naked glory. 'You're wasting your time working for the government, you know that? Anytime you feel like quitting your day job, let me know. I could get you a screen test.'

If anyone was wasting time, it was Warren Eastleigh, Jarvis thought. Now that she had committed herself, she wanted to get straight to it. No small talk, no pussyfooting around and minimal foreplay. Just good, honest, straightforward fucking.

God, she felt horny! Jarvis couldn't remember the last time she'd been so hot. Her lips felt swollen and smarting as though she'd been smacked in the mouth. Her nipples were on fire. Her stomach was churning with anticipation and her cunt, prickling with juice, positively ached to be filled with stiff cock. She threw herself at Eastleigh, slipping open the silk robe and tossing it back over his shoulders. His body was strong and muscular, deeply tanned. His finely shaped cock, already standing to proud attention, was everything she'd imagined it would be. She reached for it, wrapping her slim fingers around the thick shaft and marvelling at the sheer solidity and power of the tumescent organ. With her free hand, she pressed her fingers against his lips, silencing him. 'Just fuck me,' she breathed.

It was not an invitation to be taken lightly. Eastleigh stooped, sliding one hand under her firm buttocks and wrapping his other arm around her back. Straightening, he lifted her bodily off the ground and carried her effortlessly across to the huge circular bed which dominated the room.

They fell sideways together in a tangle of flesh. His skin felt cool against the burning heat of her own and Jarvis pressed herself tightly against him as though she could weld their two bodies into one. Her soft breasts mashed against the male hardness of his chest and she could feel his erection stiff and rod-like against her belly.

The sensation made her shiver with pleasure, filling her with the sudden need for more direct stimulation. Jarvis grasped his hand, plunging it between the creamy softness of her thighs. 'Feel me, feel how wet I am,' she urged.

His fingers slid up into the hot valley of her crotch, cupping over the downy contour of her pubic mound. Jarvis eased over more on to her back, opening her legs in submission, bestowing upon him the freedom of her most intimate self.

She was already moist in anticipation of his touch. Her swollen pussy lips parted effortlessly as Eastleigh pressed two fingers into the slippery cleft between them, encountering the hot and sensitized button of her clitoris. Her body surged in response. Something between a sob and a groan rose in her throat, finally passing out between her lips as a long, drawn-out sigh of satisfaction.

Eastleigh continued his quest of exploration, sliding his fingers over her pulsing clit and into her cunt. He began to roll his wrist in a sensuous back-and-forth motion, causing them to drill even deeper into her juicy recesses.

Jarvis groaned. 'Oh, that feels so good, so good.' She rolled completely over on to her back, the better to enjoy the stimulation of his expert finger-fucking. She reached for his beautiful prick, wrapping her hand around the thick stalk in a tightly clenched fist, feeling its throbbing hardness against her palm and fingers. With a light, delicate flexing of her wrist, she began to jerk him off with slow, lazy strokes.

It was almost enough, she thought. Almost, but not quite. The stimulation of his fingers working steadily inside her pussy and the feel of his gently pulsing cock in her hand raised her to a point of sensation which was certainly beyond simple pleasure yet just short of complete satisfaction. The effect was to split her, both physically and emotionally. On the one hand, the hungry, aching feeling deep in her cunt demanded the satisfaction of his cock inside her. On the other, she was more than content to enjoy the rippling waves of ecstasy which their mutual masturbation produced, and she wanted to make it last indefinitely. To give it up for a few minutes of frantic fucking seemed a waste. She compromised eventually, as women often do, by leaving the whole matter up to her man, letting him set the pace.

This decision itself, once made, caused her to glow with a sense of deep satisfaction. Jarvis couldn't remember the last time she had been able to give herself over so completely to a man, feel in touch with her own basic femininity, and it made her feel good. Perhaps there was more of Stella in her than she had ever realised, she thought. She continued lazily stroking Eastleigh's great cock, listening to the sounds of her own churning juices as he plunged his fingers in and out of her brimming honeypot.

She drifted in this strange limbo between desire and gratification for what seemed like an eternity. She was on a plateau of sexual pleasure she had never reached before, and it both thrilled and frightened her. Perhaps this experience was proving to be some kind of watershed, she thought – after which she would never be quite the same again. Perhaps she would never again be able to erect her protective barriers, deny the raging sexual beast which lurked behind the icy facade she projected. This was the real fear – that she would be at the mercy of men again, as she had been once before. Even more disturbing, she would be at the mercy of men like Thomas Hannah, whose image suddenly popped, unbidden and unwanted, into her mind. Just for a moment, she imagined it was his fingers probing her cunt, his cock throbbing in her hand. She shivered – unable to distinguish whether it was with rapture or with dread.

Then Eastleigh spoke, his voice jerking her back to reality. 'I'm going to fuck you now. You want that, don't you?'

She nodded, speaking and sobbing at the same time. 'Oh God, yes. I want that more than I've ever wanted anything in my life.' She felt his fingers withdraw from her cunt, his hand seeking purchase against the rounded cheeks of her ass as the other slid under her back. Unprotesting, she let him flip her over and push up her knees until she was crouched submissively. Then he was pulling himself into position behind her, the domed head of his cock poised between his thighs.

Eastleigh pressed himself against her ass, rubbing his cock against her slippery cleft to lubricate it with her flowing juices. Jarvis found herself quivering in anticipation, each passing second seeming to stretch out into an agony of waiting. The ache inside her was more pronounced now, like a severe cramp, and only the feel of his great cock surging into her hungry hole would bring any relief.

But Eastleigh had other plans. Besides being a consummate cocksman, reading women like an open book and knowing the crucial importance of good timing, he felt that he had opened a psychic link with Jarvis. He could tell she was hungry for his cock, but he knew it had to be more than that. He wanted her desperate. Instinctively, he understood that she needed it too – to be pushed to the utter limits so that she could finally throw off the last traces of her sexual reserve. Only then could the Stella trapped inside her be set free, enabling Jarvis to find her own release.

He let his cock slide along the groove between her pussy lips a few more times then held himself still, with the head of his weapon throbbing gently against her hypersensitised clit. Jarvis moaned with frustration, realising that he was teasing her but not knowing why. Desperately, she waggled her ass, thrusting backwards in an attempt to push herself over the prize which was so tantalisingly close.

A subtle movement of Eastleigh's hips, and the attempt failed. Jarvis moaned again, more urgently, and tried once more. But he was prepared for her. Matching his moves to hers, he pulled in his stomach muscles just as she might have caught the head of his cock in her hungry portal, and the teasing game continued.

Finally, as he knew it would, Jarvis's frustration reached fever pitch. Something snapped inside her. The need for his hard cock filling her yearning depths was an agonising pain, her continuing frustration a mental torture she could no longer endure. Finally, as though she was listening to someone else's voice, Jarvis heard herself pleading for the first time in her life.

'Stick it in me – please,' she begged.

'Yes.' Eastleigh's own voice was a throaty whisper. 'Yes, now you're really ready.' He took the shaft of his cock in his hand, guiding it into position.

Jarvis felt the bulbous head settle into place in the mouth of her vagina and let out a long, deep sigh of relief. Flexing her knees, she plunged her ass backwards, finally impaling herself upon the throbbing spike which she craved so much.

The pain ebbed away as she felt the passage of his thick tool in through the mouth of her cunt. Then there was only pleasure as the full length and thickness of it glided smoothly into the depths of her juicy love canal.

'Now fuck me,' she hissed. It was part plea, part command.

'Oh yes.' Eastleigh pumped his hips forward, ramming the head of his cock all the way up to the neck of her womb. Jarvis came almost at once – a rolling, surging wave of pleasure which started up somewhere deep inside her belly and found its way to every extremity of her body. Intense as the sensation was, Jarvis knew, instinctively, that it was only the start. She geared herself for one of those long, sustained orgasms which all women dream of but very few attain.

There was no teasing now. Eastleigh threw himself into full-blooded fucking, plunging in and out of her with the ferocity of a mating stud bull. Jarvis felt her whole body judder as the blunt head of his cock slammed repeatedly against the ring of her cervix like the beating of a great bass drum. In perfect time, his heavy balls slapping softly against the insides of her thighs provided the kettledrum accompaniment. It was a seductive, hypnotic rhythm, and Jarvis abandoned herself to it completely. Riding her own wave of rapturous pleasure, she climaxed three more times before Eastleigh eventually gave one last violent thrust and pumped his own small contribution into the hot liquid pool of her juices.

There was a smile of wonder on her face as Eastleigh heaved himself off and collapsed beside her. 'Was that me – or was that Stella?' she asked him.

He grinned, catching his breath. 'I'd say that was a joint effort.'

Jarvis reached for his damp, soft cock, giving it a gentle squeeze. 'The next one's going to be a solo effort,' she promised him.

EIGHTEEN

CHEYENNE, WYOMING. AUGUST 9TH. 6.32 PM.

It was a long time since Hannah had been in cowboy country and he felt out of place in his city suit. Check shirts, blue jeans and riding boots seemed to be standard uniform, spurs optional. Four out of five heads also sported stetsons – and that included the women.

The rodeo events seemed to be over for the day, but there were still a few people hanging around the stables and corral. Hannah finally found someone wearing an official marshal's armband.

'Know anything about the little incident that happened here a couple of days ago?'

The man eyed Hannah suspiciously. 'You mean that crazy blonde broad done up like a movie star?'

Hannah nodded. 'You saw her?'

The man shook his head. 'Not me. You want to talk to Deke Patterson. He's the lucky sonofabitch it happened to.'

'Any idea where I can find him?' Hannah wanted to know.

'Same place he's been ever since it happened. In the Longhorn Saloon right across the street, drowning his sorrows.'

'Drowning his sorrows? You said he was a lucky sonofabitch.' Hannah failed to understand.

The marshal grinned ruefully. 'Yeah, well Deke don't see it that way. He's real pissed off 'bout losing the championship. Been on a bender ever since. I'd be careful what you say to him, if I were you. He's a mite tetchy about it.'

Hannah took the warning seriously. 'Thanks.' He turned away, heading for the Longhorn, which really lived up to its name. Built on a raised boardwalk, with traditional swing lattice doors, the huge wooden building had all the classic features of an old Western saloon – including the life-sized carved Red Indian figure outside.

Hannah smiled to himself. Stella Devine must have felt really at home here, he thought. The place was straight out of a fifties' movie lot. He pushed the doors open and headed the bare wooden floor towards the bar.

'Deke Patterson?' he enquired of the bartender.

The man nodded to a lone figure seated at a table in the far corner. 'That's him over there. But if I was you and I was thinking about going over to talk to him, I'd take a big pitcher of beer with me.'

It seemed everyone in town was in the advice business, Hannah thought. Or maybe it was just good salesmanship. All the same, he bought a quart jug of draft Coors.

A dozen similar empty jugs already littered the table. Either Deke had a lot of visitors or he had a thirst like a mule. Hannah appraised the man as he approached.

He was young – probably no more than twenty-four, Hannah guessed – and built like the side of a barn. The rodeo marshal's warning rang in his ears. Bureau self-defence training had never included barroom brawling and Hannah didn't fancy his chances if it came to the crunch. He approached the table warily.

'Mind if I join you?' he asked politely, setting the jug of beer down on the table.

Deke looked up through bleary eyes, showing the same in-built suspicion of city folks the marshal had. 'You a newspaper feller?' he demanded.

Hannah shook his head. He considered pulling his ID but decided against it. Any sigh of officialdom would probably be like a red rag to a bull to a man like Deke. 'Just someone who wants to buy you a drink,' he lied. He pushed the full pitcher under the man's nose.

Deke refilled his glass, half emptied it again in a couple of mighty gulps and regarded Hannah sourly. 'S'pose you wanna hear about me and that movie-star dame?' he grumbled.

Hannah shrugged, trying to look – and sound – as casual as possible. 'Only if you want to tell me.'

Deke finished his beer and replenished it. 'I've told everybody else. I might as well tell you.' An expression of maudlin self-pity crept over his craggy face. 'Three whole seasons, I've been bull-riding champeen of this county. Still would be, if that blonde bitch hadn't fucked the life outta me. Weren't even fit to ride a milking cow after she'd done with me.'

It looked like it could be a long story. Hannah tried to speed things up a bit. 'Any idea why she picked on you?'

Deke shook his head sorrowfully. 'Can't rightly say – 'cepting maybe that everybody around these parts knows I got the biggest pecker in three states.'

It was a factual statement rather than a boast, but Hannah's expression must have implied disbelief. Deke's face darkened. He staggered to his feet, fumbling with the zipper on his jeans. 'You think I'm bullshittin'? Well you jest take a look at Ol' Glory and change your mind, mister.'

To back up his words, Deke proceeded to haul out

the biggest cock Hannah had ever seen. As thick as a toddler's wrist, it dangled almost to the man's kneecap. Just for a moment, Deke's truculent expression was replaced by a flash of pride. 'When that's up and runnin', most gals have to stand on a bucket to give me a blow job,' he boasted wildly.

Hannah felt some response was called for, but was at a loss for words. 'Very impressive,' he muttered, hoping it was enough.

Honour was satisfied, it seemed. Deke tucked Ol' Glory back inside his pants with a triumphant smile. 'I ain't never come across a gal before who could rightly handle it, but that blonde bitch, she managed to swallow the lot. Dangdest thing I ever did see.'

'So tell me about it,' Hannah prompted, relieved that they finally seemed to be getting down to the nitty-gritty.

Deke finished zipping himself up and drained his beer. 'Well, it was like this. I was in the back of the changing tent, just fixing to go out for my first ride of the day. Then suddenly, 'fore I knows it, this blonde is standing in front of me all dressed up in this white fur coat. Real weird, it being a hot summer's day an' all.'

'And you recognised her?'

'Hell, no. I didn't have no idea who she was, not ever seeing any of them old movies. It was only afterwards, when other folks told me she looked like this Stella Devine character. All I knew then was that she weren't no cowgirl, that was for sure.'

'And then what happened?' Hannah asked.

Deke's eyes had begun to sparkle faintly. 'Well, sir, that's when she just threw off that fur coat and she's bare-assed naked underneath. And then she looks at me real cool and says, "I want you to fuck me, cowboy." Just like that, bold as brass.'

'Go on,' Hannah prompted. Things were getting interesting.

'Well, I was real polite, you understand? I told her straight out that I'd be more than happy to oblige her later on, but right then I had to go out and ride a bull. That's when she turned real ornery.'

This was a development Hannah hadn't been prepared for. His eyes narrowed. 'How do you mean, exactly?'

'Well, she got this real determined look in her eyes, and she jest kept on coming towards me. Then she starts playing with her tits, right underneath my nose. Holding 'em up, squeezing 'em, jigging 'em about – like she's showing me what's on offer. Then she tells me flat – "You ain't riding no bull, cowboy, you're gonna be riding me." Next thing I know is she's pulling off my pants and she's got Ol' Glory and my balls in her hands.'

'And you were still resisting at this point?' Hannah asked, trying to get things straight in his head.

Deke managed a lopsided, sheepish grin. 'Well, I don't know about resisting. Ain't a lot a feller can do when someone's got hold of his nuts. All I know is that I weren't interested – and if that dumb broad had had a lick of sense she'd a knowed it by the way Ol' Glory was jest hanging his head.' He broke off to drain the last of the pitcher. 'Anyways,' he went on eventually, 'that was when she really cut loose and started bad-mouthing me, saying all sorts of dirty stuff. Man, I ain't ever heard a woman talk that way.'

'What sort of things was she saying?' Hannah interjected.

''Bout how she was gonna have my cock up her cunt whether I liked it or not. How she was gonna drain every drop of spunk I had in my balls – stuff like that. Real dirty talk.'

A snatch of the Dean Carter interview from 1957 flashed into Hannah's mind. *That Billy-Jo, she could have real dirty mouth on her sometimes...* He also pictured Stella squeezing out Critchlow's cock on the videotape, noting Deke's reference to *draining every drop of spunk*. There was a strange consistency, like a series of repetitive threads running through the entire story. None of them made any sense. He pulled his thoughts back to the present. 'So then what happened?'

'Well, sir – she jest dropped right down there on her knees in front of me and started giving Ol' Glory the full treatment. She was kissing it, and stroking it, rubbing it between her tits. She even popped the end of it in her mouth and ran her tongue right round underneath the foreskin. I'm tellin' you – I was starting to get seriously interested right about then.'

Hannah could believe it. He was tempted to make some comment, but he kept his mouth shut, not wanting to interrupt the narrative. Deke was warming to his theme now.

'So then she starts sucking my balls, pulling 'em right between her lips like they was Juicy Fruit gobstoppers. Then she's running her tongue up and down Ol' Glory, again, lickin' and kissin' it for all she's worth. Kinda knocked the last bit of fight outta me, that did. Next thing I know is I got a boner on you could split logs with. Guess you can take the rest from there, huh?'

Hannah hastened to keep the man in full flow. 'No, carry on. I'd like to hear the whole story.'

Deke's eyes narrowed. 'Hey – you ain't some kind of a pervert, are you? 'Cos if you was, I might just take it into my head to break your skull.'

Hannah laughed nervously. 'No, of course not. I just appreciate a good story, that's all.'

'Well, that's alright then.' Deke seemed mollified.

'So, there weren't much else I could do then but give the lady what she wanted. I knowed I weren't gonna be riding no bull with a hard-on like that, so I might as well make the best of it. I jest laid her out there on the floor and got right down to it. Man, I tell you now – that was the hottest piece of ass I ever had.'

There was a point Hannah needed to check. 'Earlier on, you said most girls couldn't handle your equipment, but she managed it. What exactly did you mean by that?'

Deke looked slightly embarrassed. 'Well, sir, I don't rightly know if a man should be boastful and all – but to tell you the truth of it, Ol' Glory is jest a mite too big for most of the gals I've ever knowed. I usually get to stick about half of it in before they start hollerin' about not being able to take it, if you get my meaning. But this gal – she don't even murmur as I sock it to her. Ol' Glory, he just slid into that hot sheath of hers like a Colt forty-five slippin' into a custom-made holster. I buried myself right up to my balls, and she jest lay there taking it. If I didn't know better, I'd figure that broad had a cunt that went all the way up to her belly button.'

'And was there anything else unusual about the way she made love?' Hannah wanted to know.

Deke shook his head. 'Nope. 'Cepting maybe the way she enjoyed it so much. I mean, I've knowed a few gals who like their poontang some – but this one, it was like there weren't nuthin' else in the whole wide world. She was twisting, and writhing, and heaving her ass off the floor, and kicking her legs in the air like some wild thing. I've ridden some pretty tough broncs in my time – but this little gal put 'em all to shame. And when I finally shot my sauce – she damn near went crazy.'

'After you came – did she try to squeeze out your

cock, like she was trying to get out the last drop?' Hannah asked.

Deke grinned. 'Listen, mister – when Ol' Glory shoots his load there ain't nuthin' left up the barrel, believe me.'

Hannah was disappointed. It wasn't the answer he'd wanted to hear. Just when he thought he'd started to establish some sort of a pattern, it broke down.

It was all starting to look like some crazy Chinese puzzle, where all the pieces appeared to be the same shape, but didn't quite fit.

NINETEEN

LAZY W MOTEL, CHEYENNE, WYOMING. 9.38 PM.

There were two messages waiting for Hannah when he got back to his motel. One was from Jarvis in California to say she'd be staying over another couple of days. Hannah found himself wondering if she was getting laid, and was surprised to realise there was an element of jealousy in his thoughts.

The second message was from Valerie in Florida. Since she must have gone to the trouble of contacting Bureau HQ to get his location, it sounded important. He dialled her call-back number immediately.

'Hi, Val, it's Hannah. I got your message.'

The woman sounded relieved to hear his voice. 'Hannah, thanks for calling back. Listen – something weird.'

'Weird?' Hannah's ears pricked up.

'I've been seeing these news stories – about people reporting Stella Devine sightings.'

'Yeah?' Hannah was guarded, not wanting to prompt her in any way. The original Critchlow seduction hadn't been mentioned at their last meeting. The connection with Scheller had been too new and too tenuous at the time, and it hadn't seemed important. Obviously, Valerie now thought it was.

'Well, it sort of got me thinking,' Valerie went on.

'About Carl being so obsessed with Stella and everything. So I checked through his personal computer files – and I came up with some very strange links.'

Hannah's interest was growing. 'What sort of links?'

'Well, for instance – all those free breast enhancement jobs Carl did for his little bimbo friends. I always thought they were just because he wanted to keep his hand in, maybe get a bit of young stuff on the side as a bonus. Only maybe there was a bit more to it than that.'

Hannah was completely hooked now. 'Go on.'

'There were eighteen such operations in all,' Valerie continued. 'Spread over the four years down here in Key West. Eighteen different girls, eighteen different body types – yet every one of them ended up as a perfect thirty-eight-C. Now ain't that one hell of a coincidence?'

It certainly was, Hannah thought. 'Scheller's favourite size?' he suggested. 'Or just any red-blooded guy's favourite size.'

Valerie chuckled. 'Maybe – but there's one other odd coincidence.' She paused briefly. 'Stella Devine was a perfect thirty-eight-C. So I checked a little further – and from there on in, it got even more interesting.'

She fell silent. Hannah waited expectantly for some great revelation but it wasn't forthcoming. 'And?' he prompted finally, irritably.

'And you'll have to wait for the rest until you get down here personally,' Valerie announced at last. 'Worth a little trip, don't you think? There'll be a bonus, of course – and I guess you can figure out what that'll be.'

It didn't take Hannah's full IQ potential or intelligence training to work. 'That's blackmail,' he protested, half jokingly.

The woman chuckled again. 'Yes it is, isn't it?

Terrible the things an old dame like me has to do to get laid. So – when can I expect you?'

He was caught – at least figuratively – by the balls. He gave in without a fight, justifying himself by Jarvis's little stay-over in California. If she could take a couple of extra days to stay on the job, then so could he.

'I'll catch the first available flight,' he told her. 'Should be there around mid-morning, local time.'

Valerie sounded pleased. 'Can't wait. Just hearing your voice makes me feel horny as hell. You want me to tell you some of the things I'm going to do to that beautiful cock of yours when you get here?'

Hannah grinned. 'Yeah, you do that. It'll give me something to dream about on the plane.'

TWENTY

KEY WEST, FLORIDA. AUGUST 10TH. 10.38 AM.

Hannah called Valerie from the airport to tell her he'd arrived. Stepping out from the phone booth, he glanced across the terminal towards the hire car desks. The Avis and Hertz terminals were both busy, with long lines of waiting customers, and he'd neglected to bring his Gold Card. The Dollar desk was less crowded, but Hannah had once had a bad experience over some minor fender damage, and he held grudges. He decided to take a cab instead.

Valerie was ready and waiting for him when he reached the clinic. Freshly made up and her hair brushed until it shone, she was at her gorgeous best and even younger-looking than he remembered. She started stripping off her nurse's uniform the moment he stepped through the door. She was naked underneath.

She'd already planned out her schedule of business, Hannah realised, and grinned resignedly. 'Play first, work later huh?'

Valerie nodded. 'Too right.' She moved towards him, reaching for his zipper. 'Jeezus, Hannah – I had my vibrator doing overtime all last night, knowing you were on your way.' She had his soft cock already in her hand, squeezing it lovingly before she pressed her face forwards to kiss him. Her lips were hot, trembling slightly as they clamped against his.

Hannah let her snake-like tongue invade his mouth for a long time before pulling back, sucking in a deep breath. 'Maybe you need to change the batteries,' he suggested, with a half-smile.

Valerie shook her head. 'No, what I need is *this*,' she murmured, giving his hardening cock a fresh squeeze. 'In my mouth first, I think.'

She dropped to her knees, matching action to words.

Hannah let out a long, deep sigh of pleasure as her soft, hot lips pressed against the head of his dick, her flickering tongue lapping over the taut flesh. He felt himself jerk into full erection almost immediately, a warm and contented glow spreading throughout his groin.

Valerie gave a little grunt of satisfaction, and set about sucking him off in earnest. The sheer expertise of her technique was another thing Hannah had forgotten. He squirmed with pleasure as the first three inches of his cock slid into the moist warmth of her mouth, while her cool fingers stroked slowly and sensuously up and down the rest of its length.

Her lips were pressed tightly around his thickness like a ring. She worked them rhythmically in perfect time with the ministrations of her fingers. The dual effect was electrifying. An involuntary shiver ran through Hannah's body at the sheer ecstasy of the sensation. He jerked his hips forward, embedding himself deeper into Valerie's oral cave of delights.

His eagerness seemed to spur her on to even greater efforts to administer pleasure. Her head bobbed back and forth in a fluid, sensuous motion as she fed upon his cock, using the flat blade of her hot tongue to lap furiously at the sensitive underside of its pulsing shaft. Hannah felt his blood quicken, the old familiar tingling sensation between his thighs announcing the onset of his climax. He pushed forwards again, wanting to bury himself in her cossetting mouth.

Again, Valerie read his needs immediately. She removed her fingers from the base of his cock, allowing its full length to settle into the back of her throat. She sucked harder and faster, pressing her full lips even more tightly against his rigid flesh. Her agile tongue rolled around the domed head, making Hannah groan with pleasure.

His gut tightened. The quivering in his loins became an ague. Coming was both a pleasure and a pain – the first the blessing of relief and the second the knowledge that his ecstasy was going to be over. Hannah experienced them both simultaneously, with a final convulsive shudder which sent his hot come pumping down her throat.

Valerie held his jerking cock in her mouth until it was finally still. She released it with a faint plop, planting a last affectionate kiss on the wilting shaft. She rose to her feet, smacking her lips with relish. 'God, you taste good,' she informed him.

She'd brought a fifth of bourbon into the clinic in anticipation of his visit. She poured two healthy measures as Hannah flopped into one of the office chairs. Handing him one, she perched herself on the edge of the reception desk. 'We might as well talk business now, while you're getting your strength back,' she announced.

Hannah didn't have to ask what he needed his strength back for. It was clear what Valerie's plans were. He threw back a healthy slug of bourbon, rolling it reflectively around his mouth as he framed his thoughts and questions.

'You said things got really interesting when you compared the eighteen breast jobs,' he said finally. 'What did you mean?'

'Here – I'll show you.' Valerie flipped on the computer on the desk, punching out a coded sequence. The screen flickered into life, displaying a full-frontal close-up of a woman's breasts.

'Ellie Morris, twenty-two, September nineteen ninety-four,' Valerie said. 'Now watch.' She keyed in another sequence, and the picture changed. Or rather – it *didn't* change, merely appeared to flick off and then on again. 'Shelley French, nineteen, May nineteen ninety-five.' She repeated the process nine more times, identifying each girl in turn.

Hannah was beginning to get the picture, but Valerie spelled it out for him anyway. 'They're all the same, Hannah – every single one. Not just perfect thirty-eight-Cs, but virtually identical. Shape, fullness, contour – even the angle of the nipples.' She paused, using the computer keyboard again. 'And here's the cruncher,' she announced. 'This is Stella herself. The prototype, as it were.'

There was no arguing with the visual evidence. Hannah whistled through his teeth. 'So all those operations – they were all part and parcel of Scheller's obsession with Stella. In a small way, at least, he was trying to recreate her?'

Valerie nodded. 'But I think he went further. Much further.'

Hannah's eyes narrowed. 'You mean the whole works? You think he turned another girl into a complete Stella copy?'

Valerie shrugged. 'I don't know. But I do know he tried – at least once. I found another file – something I knew nothing about. Carl must have carried out the operations on his own, in secret.'

She turned back to the computer, bringing up another picture. It was a girl's face this time. A face which still bore the scars of recent cosmetic surgery.

'April Harrington,' Valerie said. 'Nineteen years old – exactly the same age as Stella was when Carl first discovered her. Look at the changed lip line, the slight upward slant at the corners of the eyes. My guess is that this was a new Stella Devine face in the making – the first stages of an ongoing series of operations.'

Hannah studied the girl's scarred face intently. Valerie was right. A slight hollowing out of the cheeks, perhaps a minor alteration to the line of the nose, and he could be looking at a photograph of Stella. He took a few moments to let the full implications of the discovery sink in.

'You think he completed these operations?'

Valerie shook her head with a faint sigh. 'There's no way of telling. This is all the visual evidence I could find. But Carl was still involved with her up to two months ago, I've found out that much.'

This could be the much-needed breakthrough he'd been waiting for, Hannah thought, with a surge of elation. 'Is she still here in Key West?' he asked, hopefully.

Valerie smiled apologetically. ''Fraid not. She went back up to Newark, New Jersey just over two years ago.'

It was impossible to hide his disappointment. Hannah's face fell. He grasped at the one little straw he had left. 'But you said Scheller was still in contact. Don't you have an address on file?'

Valerie seemed apologetic, sensing that she had raised his hopes unduly. 'Perhaps contact was the wrong word. I don't think Carl was actually corresponding with her. But his bank statements show a regular monthly transfer of five hundred bucks to a Newark bank account in the name of April Harrington. Maybe she was blackmailing him.'

Hannah sighed with relief. The girl's bank account

number would be enough. She'd be traceable. On impulse, he jumped out of his chair and hugged Valerie tightly. 'Val, you're a little marvel.'

She smiled, pleased with herself. 'Well thank you, Hannah. Nice to know I'm appreciated. I hope you're feeling suitably grateful.'

He knew what was coming – and he was more than willing to oblige. He cupped her beautiful breasts in his hands, stroking the delicate nipples with his thumbs. 'Perfect thirty-eight-Cs, I assume?' he murmured.

Valerie chuckled. 'Now how did you guess?' Her hand dropped to his cock, caressing it lovingly. It was going to be a long, hot afternoon in Florida.

TWENTY-ONE

SANTA BARBARA, CALIFORNIA. 9.45 PM.

Jarvis sat at the bar of the Ramada Hotel, sipping at a Wicked Lady and analysing her thoughts. She felt a mild elation mixed with the vaguest stirrings of guilt about her extended stay in California, like a kid who has skipped school.

There had been some justification, of course – another Stella seduction which merited investigation. The victim – if that was the right word – had been the youngest yet, a recently graduated sociology student from UCLA. The encounter had followed much the same pattern as the previous seductions, with the exception that the kid's parents had been totally outraged and were trying to bring rape charges. Members of a very strict and uptight religious cult, they frowned on all pleasures of the flesh and felt their darling son had been violated. Since they had also forbidden him to soil himself further by describing his experience in any graphic detail, Jarvis had learned nothing.

So basically, the impromptu vacation had been mainly to spend a few more hours with Warren Eastleigh and to indulge in a sexual marathon. She had found the rare chance to throw away her normal inhibitions an intensely emotional and unsettling experience and she was still not quite sure what had happened. For two days she had behaved like a raving nymphomaniac, and enjoyed every minute of it. Now she needed time to come to terms with herself again before flying back to Washington. Like a newly freed genie, the seething sexual undercurrents of her personality were loath to be reimprisoned in their bottle. Hence the overnight stop at the Ramada. It was supposed to serve as a halfway house, a rehab centre.

The trouble was, it wasn't working as it was supposed to. Try as she might to pull her mind back to work, mental images of herself in bed with Eastleigh kept invading her thoughts. They were like a pornographic film playing inside her head – exciting and stimulating yet somehow strangely detached, as though it was all happening to someone else.

She pictured herself once more licking his cock with puppy-like devotion, totally submissive. And then in sexual aggression, straddling his belly, her knees pumping up and down as she rode his fleshy spike with no other thoughts than for her own orgasm. The image changed again – to one of complete equality, mutual pleasure seeking. The pair of them laying head to toe, his cock in her mouth, his face pressed between her thighs and his hot tongue darting back and forth over her clitoris. It seemed that together they had run through the entire spectrum of sexual orientation, fucked each other in every conceivable way that a man and woman could. She still couldn't quite believe it.

She finished her drink and ordered another – her fifth. Jarvis wasn't used to drinking cocktails, and she was already feeling slightly heady. It wasn't unpleasant, but it clouded her thoughts even further. She made a fresh mental effort to drag herself back to the job in hand.

The true identity of Stella remained a total mystery. Her original guess that it was some star-struck lookalike had been dented by Lauren's conviction that she was the genuine article. Warren Eastleigh believed she was a reincarnation. Hannah didn't appear to have any theory at all.

It was all very puzzling – and totally frustrating. Irritably, Jarvis wiped the chain of thought from her mind and tried another angle. Forget the actual identity of the woman, then. Who she was didn't matter so much as why she was doing what she was. What drove her? What was her purpose?

It was another seemingly unanswerable question, Jarvis reflected frustratedly. To know the solution she would have to get into the mind of the woman herself.

Another image of Warren Eastleigh suddenly popped into her thoughts. This time, however, it was not sexual, but of his parting words to her.

Don't ever forget again that part of Stella which is in you.

It was like a sudden, blinding revelation. Jarvis couldn't believe she hadn't thought of it before. If there *was* something of Stella inside her, then why couldn't she use it to understand? To know what drove her on her bizarre sexual quest? Even if a complete answer was too much to hope for, it might at least give her some kind of an insight. Failing even that, it gave her one last chance to hold on to her precious few days of sexual liberation and put it to some practical use.

It wasn't really a plan, more a working theory vaguely mapped out in her head. Fleshing it out into a definite course of action would take a little more time and effort. Jarvis slowed down her drinking rate, concentrating her thoughts.

Stella was apparently selecting men at random, seducing them with a single-minded dedication which took little or no account of their personal wishes. Critchlow had been forced into sex – at least in the initial stages. Once things got going, he appeared to have thoroughly enjoyed himself. Eastleigh had been a more willing participant, although he had chosen to see it as a spiritual rather than a physical encounter. Jarvis had no idea about the cowboy, and presently wasn't tempted to contact Hannah for further details. For the moment, at least, her partner had no place in the equation. The young student was the strangest case of all – for if his story was to be believed, he had put up quite a fight for his chastity before succumbing to the sex-goddess's charms.

So Stella was quite capable of varying degrees of force to achieve her desires. That was the one aspect of the whole thing Jarvis found hardest of all to understand. Why resort to such measures, when she could so easily have found a much more willing partner?

The clue to understanding *that* lay in following Stella's pattern, Jarvis realised. Suddenly, the plan fell into place. She cast her eyes around the lounge, seeking out a likely target.

There were two lone male drinkers seated at the bar. Jarvis appraised them both. The first, fiftyish, overweight and balding, was distinctly unappealing, and she rejected him fairly quickly. Stella might not be too fussy, but Jarvis was – and she would need some degree of enthusiasm if she was to carry the plan through. She couldn't remember the last time she'd flirted – or, indeed, if she ever had – and it might be harder than she anticipated.

The second man looked a far more attractive prospect. In his late thirties, well dressed and reasonably handsome, he had a healthy-looking body even if he was a bit on the short side. Taking a deep breath, Jarvis rose from her bar stool and moved along five places towards him.

The man glanced sideways as she seated herself

beside him. A knowing leer spread across his face. Jarvis didn't get a chance to try out her flirting skills, he was already way ahead of her.

'Listen, if you're a hooker, babe – forget it,' he informed her bluntly. 'I don't pay for it. But if you're a broad just looking for a good time, then you've come to the right place.'

Jarvis felt a shutter drop inside her head. Diamond-hard and solid. The guy was too easy, too eager, and too arrogant. Her blue eyes flashed ice crystals. 'Mister – you couldn't show a girl a good time if she paid you,' she hissed venomously.

She slid off the stool, turning her back on the bar. There was only one other prospect in the whole lounge. He was a nondescript sort of guy, dressed neatly but cheaply. His hair was fairish and needed cutting. He was probably about forty, Jarvis figured. Seated at a table with a half-finished beer, he looked lonely. She headed towards him.

'Hi. Look, mind if I sit with you just for a minute or so? That guy at the bar was bothering me.'

The man glanced up. He looked flustered, even embarrassed, before managing a hesitant but friendly smile. 'No – of course not.'

Jarvis sat down. 'Thanks,' she muttered, smiling back. She was silent for a moment, finally holding out her hand. 'Bonny Jarvis. And relax – I'm not a working girl.'

'Don Baker.' The man took her hand, shaking it. He relaxed a little, his smile turning to a rueful grin. 'And I couldn't afford you if you were. Not on my salary.'

Jarvis grinned back. 'Tell me about it,' she said, establishing a common bond. There was a long, thoughtful silence.

His room key was laying on the table. Room 212, Jarvis noted, relieved that he hadn't just popped into the hotel lounge for a drink. Knowing he had his own room would make things easier.

'So, you stay here often?' she asked conversationally.

Don shook his head. 'Afraid I'm usually a twenty bucks a night motel man. I'm only staying at this place because I'm meeting a potential client in the morning and I want to impress him.' He paused. 'I sell life assurance.'

Jarvis smiled inwardly. It all fitted. He looked like a guy called Don who sold life assurance. He was one of life's great strugglers. She was beginning to like him. 'I work in a real-estate office,' she lied. 'It's a hard life, ain't it?'

'Tell me about it,' Don said, suddenly looking embarrassed again as he realised he'd repeated her exact words.

Jarvis laughed – and then they were both laughing, the ice completely broken. Don told her a couple of funny stories about clients, and she invented a minor scandal about her boss and his secretary. An hour passed quite pleasantly.

Around eleven, Don started to get edgy again. He fiddled nervously with his room key. 'Well, I was thinking of turning in,' he informed her. 'It was real nice meeting with you.'

It was a strained moment, for both of them. Jarvis wondered if she ought to turn on the heavy seduction technique. She was somewhat pre-empted by Don's next words. 'Look, I guess I ought to tell you. I'm a happily married guy, and I don't mess around, if you know what I mean.'

Jarvis was caught on the hop as Don stood up. Then, with a final smile which was part apology, part regret, he was gone. She sat there for several minutes, wondering what the hell Stella would do under the same circumstances.

Out of the corner of her eyes, she noticed that the guy at the bar was still sitting there, staring at her with that same knowing leer on his face. On impulse, she jumped to her feet, strode across the lounge and took the elevator to the second floor.

She tapped lightly on the door of room 212. There was a momentary pause before Don opened it cautiously. Before he had a chance to object, Jarvis pushed her way into the room, closing the door behind her.

Don had already undressed for bed, and was clad in a pair of blue Paisley pyjamas. He regarded his unexpected visitor nervously. 'Look, Bonny – I tried to explain downstairs . . .' he started to stammer.

He was more than nervous, he was frightened. Perhaps, like millions of other American males, he'd seen the movie *Fatal Attraction* and it had scared the crap out of him, Jarvis thought. She pressed a finger to her lips. 'No complications, Don. No involvements,' she muttered calmly. 'This is just lonely guy, lonely girl stuff. Sex without strings. You don't even have to kiss me, so there's absolutely no emotional involvement whatsoever.'

She was watching his eyes carefully as the fear flickered into confusion. It was a look she recognised at once. The self-same expression had been on Professor Critchlow's face as Stella had stepped out of the mink. Jarvis felt a little buzz of elation. It was working out even better than she'd hoped. The situation was so similar, she couldn't have set it up and rehearsed it any more accurately. Even better, she was beginning to really *feel* like Stella. The Critchlow video was vivid in her mind as she advanced towards Don, mimicking Stella's moves as closely as possible.

The mink coat bit was tricky. Jarvis did the best she could with her tailored two-piece, unbuttoning the top and slipping it off before unclipping her skirt. She pulled her cotton blouse up over her shoulders, thankful that, like Stella, she never needed to wear a brassiere. There were only her white silk panties left. Jarvis hooked them down over her thighs, letting them glide down her smooth legs to the floor.

Completely naked, she posed provocatively for a few seconds, just as Stella had done. She was still watching Don's eyes, noting the first glimmerings of desire, growing slowly in intensity as though they were fitted with a dimmer switch.

Jarvis felt her own pulse quicken, and it seemed significant. She hadn't even considered her own personal sexual feelings yet, so what *was* it? she asked herself. The thrill of the chase, perhaps? Some deeply buried desire for dominance, for power? She filed the phenomenon away in a little mental drawer, to be analysed in greater detail later.

She advanced towards her quarry once again. Don seemed frozen and immobile. Her own movements were curiously unreal, as if they were in slow motion. She was reminded of the Critchlow video once more, and was struck by a feeling of dream-like unreality and detachment. It was as though the film *was* her reality, and she was both watching it and taking part in it at the same time. Her sense of actually being Stella became more powerful by the second.

She was standing directly in front of him now, the tips of her nipples almost brushing the fabric of his pyjama top. She reached down for the elasticated waistband of his trousers, pulling them down over his buttocks. Her fingers closed over his soft cock.

It was only with this actual physical contact that any feeling of personal involvement returned. Simultaneously, she was also suddenly and acutely aware of the sexual implications of her actions. She was Bonny Jarvis once more, she held a man's penis in her hand,

and she was about to have sex. A little shiver of pleasure ran through her body.

No sexual experience in her life had ever been like this. In what amounted to a complete role reversal, she was the predator, not the victim. She was totally in control of the situation, and it felt incredible. Jarvis marvelled at Don's submissiveness, his total lack of male aggression. Even the very symbol of his masculinity was in her hands – both literally and figuratively. His cock, and his sexual potency, was under her control. It was exhilarating, yet a bit awe-inspiring at the same time, engendering an odd undercurrent of responsibility. She wondered, only very briefly, if men ever felt like that in more normal circumstances. Again, she mentally shelved the thought for future consideration. Right now, she needed to concentrate on the moment, and her own personal feelings. One thing was clear above everything else. She was about to embark on a new experience in her life – and she was enjoying it.

Still holding Don's cock, she pushed him towards the bed, forcing him to step backwards out of the pyjama trousers crumpled around his ankles. With her free hand, she reached up and unpicked the buttons of his top.

There was no place left to go. The back of Don's thighs were now lodged against the side of the bed. Jarvis pressed forward gently, making her prominent nipples graze against the nakedness of his hairy chest. A faint prickling sensation rippled into the soft flesh of her breasts, like static electricity.

Trapped against the side of the bed, Don's only show of resistance was a stiffening of his leg and thigh muscles, preventing him from toppling backwards. His mouth opened, but it was not to protest. 'Why?' he muttered weakly, in a voice that was little more than a dry, husky whisper.

Why indeed? Jarvis wondered herself. She could only hope that they would both have the answer to that question very soon. She pressed forward more forcibly, breaking his balance. Don flopped backwards on to the bed, with Jarvis landing on top of him. She wriggled into a more comfortable position, giving herself room and freedom to continue fondling his cock.

It was already starting to swell now, as Don responded automatically to basic male instinct. No matter what his thoughts might be, there could be no argument against simple animal reactions. His penis was a sexual hair trigger, firing off the rest of his body. That, in turn, was subject to the erogenous contact of a woman's soft flesh against his, the delicate transference of chemical pheremones directly into his bloodstream. It was a programmed, inexorable physical process which once started, could not be stopped – and it worked to Jarvis's advantage. She felt a surge of triumph as his prick stiffened into throbbing hardness in her grasp.

She changed position again, lying on her side so that the inside of her thigh was pressed against the hardness of his hip bone. Releasing his erect manhood for a moment, she reached for his hand and thrust it into the warm valley of her groin. Trusting him to know what to do next, she took hold of his penis again and began to stroke it gently up and down. She felt herself tense, waiting for Don to take up the initiative.

His movements were tentative at first, merely a flexing of his fingers against the smooth insides of her thighs. Then, finding purpose and direction, they began to slide into the soft golden bush of her pubic hair, gently exploring the soft mound beneath.

Jarvis opened her legs wider, making it easier for him. She sighed as his fingers found the cleft between her pussy lips, pressing through into the hidden treasure beyond. She let him play there for a long while, knowing that he was re-establishing his manhood by feeling her juices begin to flow in response to his touch. Finally, when she was good and wet, and Don was beginning to frig her more aggressively, she took control once more.

Letting go of his cock, she slipped one leg over his and pushed herself up on to her knees. His fingers were still busily working away in her wet crack. Gently but forcefully, she grasped him by the wrist and pulled his hand away. Playtime was over. Now it was time for some real action.

Following what appeared to be Stella's favourite position, Jarvis heaved herself up over Don's thighs until her belly pressed against his erect cock. Rising on her knees, she positioned herself above the swollen head and rocked her hips gently from side to side as she sank down again. The tip of his prick caught between her lips and was trapped there, settling neatly into the well-lubricated entrance. Jarvis let herself down slowly, feeling the stiff rod slide smoothly into place like a perfectly tooled machine part.

It felt strange, impaling herself on the cock of a man she hardly knew, and who she had no particular thoughts for, or about. Yet it did not, as she had feared, make her feel cheap. On the contrary, the total lack of emotional involvement was quite liberating, generating its own peculiar kind of excitement. Somehow, it gave her the freedom to concentrate upon the purely physical pleasures of penetration, heightening them. In previous sexual experiences, her senses clouded by the turmoil of emotional passion, it seemed she had missed much of the sensation she was picking up now. Don's cock inside her felt longer, thicker, more powerful – even though he was not especially well endowed. The faint pulses given off by the throbbing shaft seemed more intense, passing directly into the enclosing walls of her vagina and from there throughout her entire body. Her cunt itself felt tighter and many times more sensitive than she remembered – even during her recent encounters with Warren Eastleigh.

She sat on Don's cock without moving for several minutes, the sheer intensity of these sensations pleasure enough in itself. Only when a dull, hungry ache started up deep in her gut did she feel the need for greater satisfaction.

Beneath her, Don groaned softly as she began to lift herself up and down on his stiff rod. Perhaps sensing her need to dominate, he lay quiescent, allowing her to dictate the pace and soaking up the exquisite sensations of her tight vaginal walls gliding against the shaft of his cock.

The desire to fuck for her own pleasure came upon Jarvis quite suddenly, completely unexpected. A primary orgasm rippled through her belly, making her let out a little gasp of surprise. She straightened up, arching her back and placing the flat of her hands on his legs, using them to give her greater leverage. Pumping with her arms and her knees and thrusting violently forwards with her pelvis, she rode him until her heart was pumping like a steam-hammer and her lungs were almost bursting.

Don came before she did, but she was so hot and wet she couldn't even feel the spurt of his emission. She just saw his mouth drop open and his eyes close in bliss. Above the sound of her own frantic grunting, she just heard a deep, shuddering sigh rasp out from his throat.

It was the trigger to finally send her on her way. Gritting her teeth, she put in one last feverish burst of energy and rode her orgasmic curve to the end of its parabola. Climaxing was like running full-pelt along a cliff edge and jumping over. A momentary sensation of flight, then weightlessness, then falling, falling . . .

Jarvis probably screamed. Afterwards, she couldn't remember. There was just exhaustion, and the feeling of being emptied out from the inside. She toppled sideways on to the bed, her pussy still pumping out love-juice in rhythmic little waves.

As she lay there, gasping for breath, Don spoke for the first time during the whole encounter. 'That was goddamned fantastic,' he said. He sounded grateful.

Jarvis nodded weakly. 'Yes it was, wasn't it?' She rolled over on to her back, gazing up at the ceiling and starting to replay the whole experience through in her head.

Doing so brought a strong feeling of anticlimax. With the mind of a woman, she already knew that she had learned a lot. Now, with the mind of an agent, it was time to get back to work, to analyse her experiences, sift through the wealth of information and extract the relevant data.

She cheered herself up with a philosophical thought.

Every job has its perks, Jarvis, she told herself.

TWENTY-TWO

NEWARK, NEW JERSEY. AUGUST 11TH. 10.20 PM.

April Harrington worked in a cocktail bar called the Golden Birdcage. Since the place was situated smack in the middle of the city's red-light district, it didn't take much guesswork to figure out what she did for a living. Obviously April didn't have any other benefactors like Carl Scheller.

Hannah found the place easily enough, lurking under a small and semi-functioning neon sign. Actually getting in might be a different matter, he thought, noting that the guy on the door was wider than the entrance he guarded. He looked mean.

Hannah walked straight past, stopping just round the corner of the block and glancing around cautiously to make sure there was no one lurking about. He pulled out his bill-fold and extracted several loose, small-denomination notes, tucking them in his jacket pocket. It didn't look like a good area to be seen waving real money about.

The burly doorman scowled at him as he returned, running his eyes up and down his well-cut suit. 'You slumming or something, mister?'

Hannah forced a smile. 'Local colour.'

The joke wasn't appreciated. 'Twenty bucks,' the doorman demanded, thrusting out a ham-like hand.

Hannah paid up without protest. Still eyeing him suspiciously, the doorman kicked the door open with his heel and allowed Hannah to descend a flight of bare wooden steps.

Inside, the Golden Birdcage was everything Hannah had expected it to be. Small, seedy, dimly lit and reeking of cigarette smoke, alcohol and cheap perfume. Suspended from the ceiling was the feature which had given the place its name. Looking more like a scrapped monkey enclosure from the city zoo than a birdcage, a large steel-barred contraption housed a pair of semi-naked girls who writhed sluggishly in vague time with the piped background music. Once painted gilt, it now appeared more of a greenish-brown colour.

A couple more topless dancers performed on a small raised dais to one side of the bar, occasionally stepping down and moving between the tables, relieving the all-male clientele of small-denomination bills which they promptly stuffed down the front of their G-strings. It was the sort of place where fifty bucks would probably get you a blow job under the table, Hannah figured, resolving not to put this theory to the test. He made his way to the bar. He ordered a straight Scotch, which cost five dollars. Hannah was glad he hadn't asked for a mixer. He handed the barman a twenty, waiving the change with a flick of his wrist. 'Maybe you can help me. I'm looking for a girl called April Harrington.'

The barman stuffed the bill in his pocket, nodding his head down the bar. 'That's April – second from the end.'

Hannah could only catch her in profile, but what he saw both surprised and deflated him. He had been expecting a blonde Stella lookalike. The woman the barman pointed out had jet-black, shoulder-length hair and, even under the heavy make-up, didn't look remotely like a movie star unless you counted Vampira. There was another inconsistency. April Harrington was supposed to be in her early twenties. The dim lights didn't help, but this woman could easily be twice that. One thing was immediately clear – April was not the woman going around the country masquerading as Stella Devine.

Hannah felt cheated. It had only been a long shot, but he'd been really hoping for a breakthrough. He swallowed his disappointment as best he could. She might still be of help in some other way. He climbed off his bar stool and sauntered over to her. 'April Harrington?'

She was staring down at the bar, fingering a dry martini. She didn't look up. 'Two hundred bucks, all night. I don't do quickies.'

'Actually, I just wanted some information,' Hannah told her.

April let out a short, cynical laugh. 'Then try the local library. I'm a working girl, mister. No pay, no play.'

Hannah thought for a minute, finally giving a resigned shrug. 'OK.' He could work out how to put this particular tab down on his expenses sheet later.

The girl finally looked at him. Full-face, Hannah could see that she wasn't quite as haggard as he'd first thought. It was the thickness of her make-up which added years to her face. It looked like she applied foundation with a plasterer's hawk. 'Let's see the money. I wanna be sure you got it.'

Hannah shook his head. 'Not here, babe. I'd like to get out of this place in one piece.'

April shrugged. 'Please yourself.' She returned her attention to the bar and her drink.

One of the topless dancers must have been watching, figuring out an angle for herself. She shimmied over, shaking her huge tits in Hannah's face. 'You fancy something more immediate, mister, we got a room out back,' she informed him. 'Twenty-five bucks for a hand job, fifty for head.'

Hannah pulled another twenty from his pocket, rolled it into a tube and stuck it in the girl's mouth. 'Suck that for free,' he muttered curtly. 'I'm busy right now.'

The obscenity the dancer threw at him was muffled by the bill between her lips. She flounced off, looking for a more cooperative customer.

April looked up from the bar again. 'OK, so you got a few bucks to throw around. You still on for two hundred?'

Hannah nodded. 'Just as long as it isn't a room out the back.'

April threw down the rest of her drink, sliding off her stool. She took Hannah's arm possessively. 'We'll go back to my place – it's only a couple of blocks from here.' She smiled, suddenly looking more like her actual years. 'I'll even treat you to the cab fare.'

Hannah took her up on the offer, letting her drag him towards the exit. He was already down fifty dollars, and the big pay-off was yet to come.

April's apartment reflected her status as a two-hundred-dollars-a-night call girl. Judging by the quality of the furnishings, she didn't go short of clients. She ushered him into the living room, pointing towards a large leather couch. 'Make yourself at home. I'll just go and change into something more comfortable.'

'Don't bother,' Hannah said. 'Like I told you, I'm only after information.'

April waved the objection aside. 'Who said it was for your benefit?' She disappeared into the bedroom, emerging a few moments later wearing only a silk wrap, undone all the way down the floor. It flapped open as she moved, giving tantalising glimpses of her naked body which Hannah found rather reassuring. The hair might be black, the face not what he had expected but the tits were one-hundred per cent pure Carl Scheller.

She perched herself on the couch beside him. 'You got the money?'

'Sure.' Hannah retrieved his bill-fold and peeled out a matched pair of C-notes. He waited as she carried the money over to a small wall safe, locked it away and returned. 'Now, let's talk about Carl Scheller.'

April's eyes suddenly blazed. She jumped to the far end of the couch, regarding him with a sullen, guarded look on her face. 'What do you know about that bastard?'

Hannah shrugged. 'Only that he's gone missing. Disappeared without a trace.'

A thin smile of triumph flitted across April's lips. 'Good. I hope he's dead.'

Hannah was surprised at her reaction. 'You hated him that much?'

The girl gave a vehement nod. 'Damn right.'

The statement begged the obvious question. 'Enough to kill him yourself?'

April faced him squarely. 'Sure, if I'd had the chance. But I didn't – get the chance *or* kill him,' she added quickly.

Hannah took the flat denial at face value. The girl didn't look as though she was lying. 'So how come you wanted him dead?' he asked after a while. 'The golden eggs die with the goose, you know.'

April shrugged. 'You mean the five hundred bucks? Fuck it. That was his idea, not mine.'

Again, Hannah was surprised. 'You weren't blackmailing him?'

April shook her head. 'He suggested that himself. It

was supposed to be hush money – to make sure I kept my mouth shut.'

'About what?' Hannah wanted to know.

An expression of deep bitterness spread across the girl's face. She raised the flat of her hand to her cheek, wiping off some of her make-up. 'About this,' she muttered, turning that side of her face towards him.

Suddenly, Hannah understood her need for such heavy cosmetics. It must take a lot of foundation to cover up the thin blue scar which ran all the way from one corner of her mouth up to her cheekbone. Jagged and ugly, it also helped to explain why she plied her trade in a dimly-lit joint like the Golden Birdcage. Facial disfigurement wasn't the best advertisement for a hooker.

Hannah looked sympathetic. 'Scheller did that?'

April shook her head again, pulling the same thin, bitter smile. 'Oh no – not the great Carl Scheller. He didn't make mistakes like that. This was done by the cheap backstreet butcher I paid to put me back the way I was supposed to look.'

Hannah wasn't sure he understood. 'Why?'

'Because I didn't fancy spending the rest of my life looking like a dead movie star. Because I wasn't willing to be a walking billboard for a crazy man's obsession.'

'You mean Stella Devine?' Hannah prompted gently.

April nodded. 'I didn't even understand what he was doing until the whole series of operations were finished. Then, when the bandages finally came off, I realised how fucking crazy he really was. He was trying to recreate his moment of glory – at my expense. And now he's gone and done it to some other poor bitch. Maybe *she* killed him.'

Hannah's ears pricked up. The girl sounded as though she knew something or at least suspected it. He approached the subject warily, careful not to feed her anything. 'Who exactly are you talking about?'

'Why, this other Stella Devine lookalike who's running around screwing guys,' April said simply. 'Hookers do read newspapers, you know.'

Hannah conceded the point. 'You think Scheller repeated his experiment on you with some other girl? And that she might have killed him?'

April flashed him a savage grin. 'Or maybe she's found an even more subtle way of making the bastard suffer,' she suggested.

'Such as?'

The girl was silent for a moment. 'Well, let's assume that I was her,' she muttered thoughtfully. 'Considering how he felt about his precious Stella, wouldn't it really make his guts squirm if he knew she was whoring about the way she is? That his perfect and adored creation was getting herself fucked all over the place just to show him how much she despised him?'

It was an angle Hannah had never even considered. It had taken another woman's viewpoint to bring it out. And it was sufficiently convoluted and bitchy to hold water. *Hell hath no fury*, he thought. There was only one little problem.

'But Scheller's not around to get the benefit,' he pointed out. 'He's disappeared.'

There was a wicked glint in April's eyes. 'That's just my point. Suppose she's got him stashed away somewhere? Locked up, unable to escape? But he'd know what's going on, and be completely unable to do anything about it? She'd have the pathetic bastard crawling up the walls, wouldn't she? Now *there's* revenge for you!'

It was quite a scenario. Hannah thought about it for a long time, trying to put himself in Scheller's shoes just as April had assumed Stella's. The more he considered it, the more it made sense. April was right – it was a pretty effective way to make a man suffer. And possibly one that only a woman could have come up with.

The only apparent fly in the ointment was Marylou Vacarro. She'd been with Scheller when he disappeared. If her story was to be believed, they had been completely alone.

But perhaps she was lying, Hannah theorised. What if she'd actually been an accomplice? He took the idea one step further, thinking of Valerie. As a rejected lover, she was another woman with her own reasons to hate Carl Scheller. Suppose there was a whole conspiracy of vengeful women out there somewhere who had chosen to deal with the man in their own way? He shivered in empathy.

'Anyway, that's my theory, for what it's worth,' April said, interrupting his thoughts before they became paranoid. She shifted her position on the couch, causing the silk wrap to sag open even more. Whether by accident or design, it got Hannah's attention. He found himself staring at the proud swell of her beautiful breasts.

'Which by my reckoning, leaves quite a bit of change out of two hundred bucks,' April went on. 'So are you ready to play yet? You already paid in advance.'

Hannah smiled awkwardly. 'Thanks, but I'll pass,' he muttered. 'Just count the change as an extra-large tip.'

He expected the girl to shrug the matter off there and then, but she didn't. In fact, she looked quite disappointed. 'Hey, don't think you're doing me any favours, mister,' she complained. 'You're a good-looking guy. I don't get many of them in my line of work. How about giving a girl a decent break, huh?'

It was a new twist, which threw Hannah off guard. He'd never come across a hooker pleading for a screw before. He made the fatal mistake of thinking about it.

From then on, he didn't have a chance.

Like a cat, April abruptly pounced across the couch towards him, leaving the wrap behind her. The weight and impetus of her naked body threw him sideways, pinning him down. With the girl's tits swaying temptingly in front of his face, resistance suddenly seemed rather pointless.

'Well, maybe just a quickie,' he murmured weakly.

April gave him a lascivious grin. 'I told you – I don't do quickies. This is a value-for-money establishment.'

She was undoing his pants as she spoke. Her fingers felt cool as they slipped through his open zipper and into the warmth of his crotch. She had a nice touch, Hannah thought, as she cupped his balls and soft cock in the palm of her hand and began teasing the whole set out over the top of his shorts.

He was lost, and knew it. Sighing with resignation, he reached up to grasp her dangling breasts, spreading his fingers around the smooth contours of each soft and perfectly shaped hemisphere.

April made a little chuckling sound in her throat. 'You like, huh?' she purred. 'That's the one part of Scheller's work I didn't get changed back.'

It had been a wise decision. Gratefully, he continued fondling the twin treasures as April's nimble fingers coaxed his dick into throbbing stiffness. She'd obviously learned a few tricks of her trade, he thought, anticipating the delights yet to come.

Minutes later, as the warm softness of her lips closed over the head of his cock, he knew he wasn't going to be disappointed.

TWENTY-THREE

BUREAU HQ, WASHINGTON, DC. AUGUST 12TH. 9.05 AM.

It was summing up time. Jarvis sat at her desk, with Hannah opposite. Between them, the desk-top was littered with their case notes.

'So, what do we have so far?' Jarvis said, starting the ball rolling. 'Four separate Stella incidents, spread out across the entire country, and with nothing apparently in common.'

'Five, actually,' Hannah put in, bringing her up to date. Untypically, Jarvis had been strangely distracted since her return from California. Equally untypically, he hadn't asked her why directly, although he was working on other ways of obtaining the information. 'Another report came in last night – a Texan oil billionaire in Houston.'

Jarvis cast a quick but professional eye over the report as he handed it to her, accepting the update with a brief nod. 'OK, five. A university professor, a rodeo rider, a Hollywood movie star, a student and a businessman. Absolutely no common factor between any of them except that they were all male.'

Hannah shrugged. 'Maybe we're wasting our time looking for a connection,' he suggested. 'Perhaps there isn't one. Maybe our Stella chooses her subjects completely at random.'

There was an obvious flaw in this argument, which Jarvis hastened to point out. 'Then why the hell is she travelling thousands of miles in between? If she just wanted to get laid five times she could do it in one town.' She paused, shaking her head. 'No, there *must* be a common link. We're just not seeing it.'

'So let's try to look at it through Stella's eyes,' Hannah suggested. 'Maybe the common factor is only apparent to her.'

Jarvis thought of her own attempt to do exactly the same thing. She couldn't fault Hannah's thinking. 'OK, then let's start with her basic motivation,' she agreed. 'How do you read it?'

Hannah thought for a moment. 'Well, if we discount April Harrington's vengeful patient theory for the moment, let's just assume that she's some sort of nympho. That also fits the pattern of the original Stella, which helps.'

Jarvis wasn't totally convinced, but for the moment was willing to go along with the idea. 'Alright – but why these particular men?'

'Big dicks,' Hannah announced triumphantly. 'My guess would be that she seeks out guys who are particularly well endowed in the marriage tackle department.'

Jarvis cast him a sceptical, patronising smile. 'And on what exactly do you base this inspired piece of lateral thinking?'

Hannah let the sarcasm wash over him. 'Well, we've got video evidence that Critchlow was pretty well hung,' he went on. 'And our rodeo rider friend claims the biggest wanger in three states – with some justification, I might add.'

'What justification?' Jarvis wanted to know.

Hannah looked sheepish. 'He showed it to me.'

Jarvis grinned, enjoying his obvious embarrassment.

'Well, Hannah, you really surprise me. I never realised you were so much into the male bonding thing. But do go on.'

Again, Hannah ignored the little barb. He was getting geared up to deliver one of his own. 'Well, that's two out of the five already.' He paused, eyeing his partner covertly. 'So what about Warren Eastleigh? Is he especially well hung?'

He was fishing, and Jarvis knew it. She faced him squarely, a bland look on her face and her blue eyes as innocent as a new-born babe's. 'I haven't the faintest idea,' she lied. 'And since neither the Texan oil-man or the UCLA student submitted to the slide-rule-down-the-trouser test, I figure that rather blows your theory out of the window.'

Hannah's little scheme to find out about the California trip had failed. He admitted defeat. 'Yes, I suppose it does,' he muttered, sounding totally deflated.

Jarvis was looking thoughtful now. 'Mind you,' she murmured. 'Your little story about Bronco Billy and his giant dipstick has got me thinking. Reigning national champion of something, wasn't he?'

Hannah nodded, frowning at the same time. 'Bull-riding. But I don't see what that's got to do with anything.'

'Don't you?' Jarvis's eyes were sparkling as her own theory took shape. 'Warren Eastleigh was twice voted the country's most handsome man. Professor Critchlow is reputed to be one of the world's leading experts in the field of biochemistry. The student graduated *summa cum laude* with the highest pass mark in his year class. And our oil-man heads up the biggest conglomerate in the state of Texas.' She paused for effect. 'Don't you get it now? Every one of them is the best of something, or top of their particular tree. *That's* the connection. Stella is deliberately seducing the cream of the country's manhood.'

Hannah whistled through his teeth, genuinely impressed with his partner's deductive powers. She was right, of course. Jarvis had hit the nail squarely on the head. But why? The question remained, and he voiced it.

Jarvis shrugged. 'That I don't know,' she admitted. 'But at least it tells us why she covers such vast distances between encounters. She's obviously targetting specific people – which means she's also probably got a route map already plotted out.'

Her enthusiasm was infectious. 'Which gives us a much better chance of tracking her than if she was striking at random,' Hannah put in. 'A couple more victims and we might even be able to get one jump ahead of her.'

Jarvis was already pulling a national map out of her drawer and unfolding it on the desk-top. She traced Stella's path to date with her finger. 'Massachusetts, Wyoming, California and Texas. East coast to west coast in one trip – and now it looks as though she's on her way back. The question is – back to where? We haven't the faintest idea where she started out from,' she concluded despondently.

'Or what sort of transport she's using,' Hannah put in. 'But maybe that's where we ought to be looking. Airports, Greyhound terminals, car-rental agencies, gas stations, diners – all the places a long-distance traveller is likely to show up.'

Jarvis brightened. 'Hannah, you might just have cracked it. She's not exactly the inconspicuous type, after all. Somebody, somewhere has got to notice her.'

Hannah didn't want to dampen her spirits, but it was necessary. 'Which still leaves us with one outstanding problem,' he said. He told her about Pepper and the man's not-so-veiled threats.

Jarvis didn't appear to see an immediate problem. 'Can't Stone call him off?'

Hannah shook his head. 'I've already tried. He claims he's never heard of the guy and has no idea who he might be working for. To tell you the truth, I was rather hoping you might be able to come up with something.'

'Such as?' Jarvis was guarded.

'Such as one of those private sources you seem to use from time to time,' Hannah said.

Jarvis had no doubt that he was alluding to Lovelace. Briefly, she wondered if Hannah actually knew more than he let on. It was not a pleasant thought. She made no reply for several minutes, her thoughts racing. Caught between a rock and a hard place, she had a difficult decision to make. In essence, it appeared to be a choice between compromising her partner's safety or making a personal sacrifice. Neither was very appealing.

'Well?' Hannah prompted, after a while.

With a sinking feeling, Jarvis realised that the idea of choice had been an illusion. There *was* no option at all. It was the primary, if unspoken law of the Bureau. Next to an Agent's own, a partner's life was sacrosanct.

'I'll see what I can do,' she said to Hannah, trying not to let him see how deeply upset she was.

She returned to her private thoughts, depressing as they were. If anyone was likely to know anything about Pepper and the secretive organisation he worked for, then it was Lovelace. Whether he was in a position to exert any influence was a different matter. And even if he could, he would expect an especially high price for a favour of that magnitude.

So far, she'd submitted to every depraved sexual act the bastard could think up short of actually letting him fuck her. She'd always drawn the line at that. This time, Lovelace might not be prepared to stay behind it.

Jarvis felt her guts tightening up just thinking about it.

TWENTY-FOUR

THE PASSION PALACE, WASHINGTON, DC. AUGUST 15TH. 8.50 PM.

Lovelace always insisted on some bizarre venue for their clandestine meetings – usually a sleazy strip joint or a cat house – but a porno movie theatre was a first. Smarting with embarrassment, Jarvis paid for her ticket at the pay booth, uncomfortably aware of the salacious looks she was getting from the rest of the exclusively male clientele.

The feature movie – *Slut Sisters* – was already playing as she walked into the darkened auditorium. Jarvis wrinkled her nose in disgust at the unmistakable and overpowering smell of stale come which filled the place. On the screen, two Puerto Rican girls lay curled up on their sides in a head-to-toe position on a large fur rug. Mouths glued against each other's cracks, they tongued each other greedily as two kneeling men pumped their oversized cocks in and out of the girls' asses.

Classic stuff, Jarvis thought cynically as she made her way to the back row of the left-hand aisle where Lovelace was waiting for her.

As expected, he already had his cock protruding from his flies and was jacking it off in a two-handed grip. He tore his eyes only momentarily from the screen as Jarvis sat down beside him, treating her to a sickly smile. 'Watch this next bit,' he hissed. 'It gets me every time I see it.' He returned his attention to the movie as the two girls rose to their knees, pressed their bright red mouths together and let each man in turn slide his cock in and out of the wet tunnel formed by their joined lips.

It wasn't something Jarvis wanted to see, despite Lovelace's exhortation. She stared fixedly at the back of the seat in front of her instead, unable to ignore the blotchy white stains of dried semen on the red velour. Feeling totally wretched, she waited for Lovelace to make his expected demand for a blow job.

It didn't come. He continued playing with himself as though she wasn't even there. Wheezing and grunting, he brought himself to a spurting climax, adding his own contribution to the unique seating colour scheme. He wiped his fingers off on the armrest, letting his prick dangle between his thighs as he turned in Jarvis's direction again.

Here it comes, she thought with a sense of foreboding. *The sick little shit is going to ask me to lick it clean then suck it back to life again.*

Instead, Lovelace was silent, a strange, hesitant look in his eyes. Almost as if he was waiting for her to make demands, Jarvis reflected. It was all rather odd, and she didn't understand. The man was acting completely out of character. It seemed like a good time to press her luck. 'Well – did you manage to do what I asked?' she whispered.

Lovelace gave a nervous little cough. 'Maybe yes, maybe no,' he muttered thickly. 'It depends.'

'On what?'

'On how you and your partner pursue your investigation from here on in,' Lovelace expanded. 'I can't buy you any protection if you carry on digging out old files.'

'On Stella Devine?' Jarvis pressed.

'On anything which isn't directly to do with the Scheller case. Stick with that, and stick to the present – that's all I can tell you.' He fell abruptly silent, watching the movie again.

Jarvis studied his face in profile. He didn't seem to be enjoying it. In fact, he looked distinctly strained.

The man was rattled, Jarvis realised suddenly. More than that – he was scared. She wasn't sure whether this discovery should give her cause for enjoyment or trepidation. What she did feel sure about was that he was vulnerable enough to be pushed.

'I need more, Lovelace,' she hissed insistently. 'Just who are we dealing with here?'

The man's discomfiture was more obvious now. There was a definite nervous twitch pulling at the corner of his mouth as he spoke again. His tone carried a strong element of warning – and something more. If she hadn't known better, Jarvis might even have taken it for friendly concern. 'Just leave it, Bonny – for both our sakes. These guys don't mess around and they play rough, believe me.'

He wasn't going to be pushed much further, Jarvis could tell. For once in his nasty little life, Lovelace had come up against something he couldn't manipulate or control, and it had shaken him to the core.

'Just give me one lead – a name, even,' she demanded.

Lovelace chewed at his bottom lip for a while, finally sighing heavily. 'Alright – one name,' he conceded wearily. 'Then you leave me alone and no more contact unless I approach you.'

'Agreed,' Jarvis said without hesitation. Anything which would keep Lovelace at arm's length was fine by her.

'Jerome – Walter Jerome.'

The name rang faint bells in Jarvis's head, but she couldn't quite put her finger on why. She considered pressing Lovelace one more time but one glance at his face was enough to tell her he had finally clammed up for good. His mouth was closed and compressed into a thin line as though he had stuck his lips together with superglue. His eyes were fixed blankly on the movie, where the two male characters had been joined by a third and were fucking one of the girls in all three available orifices simultaneously.

Jarvis rose to her feet, getting ready to leave. Four seats further along the row from Lovelace, an effeminate-looking youth was suddenly looking interested. He moved towards Lovelace as Bonny moved away, taking the seat next to him and dropping his hand over the armrest and into the man's lap. There was no resistance.

By the time Jarvis reached the aisle and took a quick glance back, he was already kneeling between the seats and licking Lovelace's cock like a pet dog. Still staring at the screen, the man didn't seem to notice.

Even with the ever-present reek of city traffic fumes, the air outside the movie house seemed sweet by comparison. Jarvis sucked in several deep breaths gratefully, clearing her lungs and her mind at the same time. Suddenly, she recalled why the name Lovelace had given her had rung bells.

Walter Jerome was the NASA scientist who had disappeared a year before Carl Scheller.

TWENTY-FIVE

LOUIE'S GYM, LAKE CHARLES, LOUISIANA. AUGUST 17TH. 3.46 PM.

Louie watched his protégé finishing up a hundred faultless press-ups with a grin of satisfaction. If ever he had been lucky enough to have a real contender for the Mr Universe title under his control, then it was Wayne Patterson. Six foot one, a hundred and ninety-eight pounds of solid muscle, he was as near physical perfection as man could get. He already held the Southern States Body-Building Championships belt and the National Adonis title. Now he was in training for the big one.

Patterson completed the final press-up and bounded to his feet, running on the spot to keep his heart pumping. He was at the very peak of fitness, Louie thought. A full hour of work-out had hardly taxed him at all. His ebony body glistened with sweat, yet he didn't even appear to be breathing heavily. Still, there was no point in overdoing things.

'OK, let's call it a day,' Louie said. 'You've done enough.'

Patterson grinned, flashing a set of white teeth which would have put a Steinway piano to shame. 'You go ahead and close up, Louie. I just want to do a few weights and then I'm through. I'll lock up as I let myself out.'

The man was a glutton for punishment, Louie thought, frowning slightly. But it was precisely that sort of dedication which was going to make him a winner. He couldn't argue with that. 'Alright, but just don't overdo things, OK?'

'Sure.' Patterson moved across the gym and picked up a set of barbells. He began swinging them rhythmically, making his mighty biceps bulge like oven-ready chickens. With a faint shake of his head, Louie left him to it.

Patterson heard the outside door slam and speeded up his rhythm, rolling his head around at the same time to exercise his neck muscles. Now he was on his own he could really push himself. Louie was a good trainer, but he tended to be a bit soft.

'You heard what your trainer said – you've done enough for today,' a soft female voice purred behind him.

Patterson was taken by surprise. Lowering the barbells, he pivoted on the balls of his feet to face the gorgeous blonde standing just inside the locker-room door. She was completely naked, a white mink coat lying on the gym floor at her feet. His mouth dropped open. He was used to seeing perfect male bodies, but this babe made the average woman look like a stick insect. She was built like a movie star, he thought. Then, looking more closely at her face for the first time, it hit him. She *was* a movie star!

Stella smiled. 'Besides, I got some better exercises in mind for you,' she said. 'Why pump iron when you could be pumping me?'

Patterson gaped at her dumbly as she moved towards him and he noted the fluid swing of her flaring hips, the faint bounce of her swelling breasts. This couldn't really be happening, he told himself. Maybe Louie was right, and he'd overdone things. He was suffering from some bizarre effect of hyperventilation or adrenaline rush. He blinked – several times – but the image didn't go away.

Stella moved in close, the smell of her perfume driving away the stench of his own sweat from his nostrils. She reached down to grasp his hands, prising the two barbells from his fingers and dropping them to the floor. Her fingers moved to his lower abdomen, tearing away his briefs and posing pouch in one snatch. Her long eyelashes fluttered as she glanced down at the prize she'd exposed.

'Nice,' she murmured appreciatively. 'Good to see it's not just your muscles which are well developed.' She scraped her long pointed fingernails under the wrinkled sac of his scrotum, bringing her hand up slowly until his soft cock nestled in her fingers.

'So, just a few questions, and we can get down to those special exercises I was talking about,' Stella murmured. 'You *would* like to fuck me, wouldn't you?'

There wasn't a trace of saliva left in his mouth or throat, but Patterson swallowed anyway. An hour of heavy work-out hadn't made him breathe heavily, but now he was beginning to pant slightly. A shiver of anticipation rippled through his muscular frame.

He'd never had a white woman before. It was nothing whatsoever to do with ideas about racial purity, simply that the opportunity had never presented itself. Now here it was on a plate. The thought made him feel nervous.

'Questions?' he managed to stammer out. 'What sort of questions? I ain't got no diseases or nothing like that, if that's what you mean.'

Stella smiled reassuringly. 'Of course you haven't. Otherwise I wouldn't have chosen you. It's just that I'm a little concerned about drugs.'

Patterson shook his head in denial. 'No, ma'am – I

ain't into anything like that. A little grass sometimes – but nuthin' heavy.'

'Steroids, hormone treatments?' Stella enquired politely. 'I understand some of you body builders use things like that.'

Patterson shook his head again. 'No ma'am. Just protein concentrates – all natural stuff.'

Stella looked pleased. 'Good. We can't afford any contaminants. Purity is essential.'

Patterson didn't have the faintest idea what she was talking about, but he didn't care. His cock felt hot and throbbing against the coolness of her fingers, and the thought of slipping it into her creamy, perfect body was about the only thing left in his mind which seemed to have any importance or make any sense.

Stella was casting her eyes around the gym. 'Now, where shall we do it?' she mused aloud. 'I fancy something different, something a bit fun. All this straight fucking gets a bit stale after a time.'

She appeared to be talking to herself, Patterson thought. It occurred to him that she might be just the slightest bit crazy, but he wasn't prepared to argue about it. His manhood was so hard it ached. He was quite happy to fuck her anywhere she fancied and in any position – just so long as it involved his cock being between the lips of her beautiful golden-fringed cunt.

Stella's eyes finally lighted on the wall bars at the back of the gym, and sparkled with delight. 'Perfect,' she breathed. 'We'll go for the Saint Catherine variation.'

Patterson still had no idea what she was on about, but he followed her over to the wall bars. He watched, fascinated, as Stella backed up to them and pulled herself up off the floor. Then, stretching her arm upwards and outwards, she locked them behind one of the highest bars and opened her legs wide until she looked for all the world like a sacrificial victim crucified against the spokes of a giant wheel. Grinning down at him, she thrust her pelvis out provocatively. 'All yours, my fine and muscular friend.'

It didn't take much figuring out to get the idea. Patterson stepped forward, holding his erect cock out like a lance. Stella couldn't have picked a more suitable height at which to suspend herself. Her stretched pussy lips were like a little pink target, on a direct line with the head of the approaching dick.

He was sorely tempted to drop to his knees and tongue her first. It might be interesting to find out if vanilla pussy tasted any different to the chocolate flavour he was used to. But his prick was throbbing painfully, demanding priority treatment. Patterson decided to satisfy it.

He eased himself into her warm cleft, holding his dick up at a slight angle. One gentle push forward, and he was inside her, feeling the liquid heat of her vagina against his sensitive frenum. Grasping the wall bars, he pulled himself close against her lush body.

Patterson was amazed at the ease with which the shaft of his cock slid into her silky sheath. There had been no foreplay, and yet she felt as wet and ready for sex as any woman he had ever been with. It was almost as if she was perpetually primed for that pastime alone. He let out a low moan of pleasure as he sank into the delicious tunnel of love up to his balls.

With her legs stretched so widely apart, Patterson had feared that she might feel too slack and loose, but he was pleasantly surprised. The juicy walls of her cunt were like a soft vice around the shaft of his cock, encasing it in soft, slippery and faintly pulsating flesh. He had the strong suspicion that she could probably bring him to orgasm if he just left his prick where it was and didn't make a single in or out stroke. It was something he would like to have tried, but he prided himself as a great cocksman. The fortunate combination of his generously proportioned cock, sexual technique and sheer physical stamina meant that he could raise most women to a frenzy of erotic stimulation, and the blonde would be no exception. She was expecting some good hard fucking – and by God he was going to give it to her!

He ground his pelvis against hers, screwing himself into her tunnel-like depths and grinning triumphantly. 'Enough meat for you, baby?'

There was a quiet, secretive and faintly mocking smile on Stella's perfectly shaped lips. 'That'll do for starters, big boy. Now what you got for the main course?'

Patterson took it as a direct challenge. His mighty abdominal muscles rippling with latent power, he pulled back until the head of his cock almost popped out of her juicy cleft. Then, jerking his hips forwards, he plunged back inside her with a savage, powerful thrust which made the wall bars rattle.

Stella's eyes rolled in ecstasy and an appreciative grunt was forced out from between her lips. She pushed her own pelvis forward, swallowing his entire length and still leaving room for more. The softness of her belly slapped against the muscular hardness of his, her lush breasts spilling over his shoulders.

Patterson pulled hard against the bars, trying to drive the last centimetre of his bone-like erection into her demanding cunt. The woman seemed insatiable, her pussy a deep and hungry tunnel seemingly without end. Fired with male ego, he rocked himself against her suspended body, his cock now completely engulfed.

Stella changed her tactics abruptly, dropping her legs from their spread-eagled position and locking her knees tightly together. Internal muscles came into play, squeezing the fleshy walls of her pussy around the throbbing shaft buried inside her. Little rippling sensations of pleasure coursed up and down its full length.

Patterson groaned, feeling the exquisite manipulations of her agile cunt against his rigid flesh. She was like no woman he had ever known before, seemingly able to massage his cock from the inside as though she had her own in-built vibrator. His prick had never felt so hard or throbbed so violently. The total effect was that of pleasure and pain both raised to a point of near bliss.

Patterson felt almost delirious with pleasure. It was her doing the fucking now, not him – but it didn't seem to matter. All ideas of sexual dominance had suddenly disappeared from his mind. No longer harbouring the slightest inclination to play the sexual stud, he abandoned himself to the unique intensity of the experience.

That appeared to suit Stella just fine. She writhed against his tightly pressed body, making little purring noises deep in her throat. She tightened her stomach muscles again, increasing the tightness of her vaginal walls against his imprisoned cock. Flexing and unflexing, she squeezed against the pulsing shaft as though to suck out its precious juices.

Fearing that she would bring him off prematurely and put an end to the delicious pleasure, Patterson dared only to make a few gentle side-to-side movements with his hips. It was a mistake, he realised almost immediately. With Stella already thrusting against him and the continued manipulations of her incredible cunt, he almost shot his bolt there and then. It took a considerable mental effort to pull back from the brink, but he finally managed it. Much relieved, he concentrated his thoughts on prolonging the pleasure once more.

But Stella had other ideas. She released her grip on the wall bars suddenly, throwing her arms around Patterson's bull-like neck as she fell. Her slim legs arched up and around his back, locking themselves into position over his buttocks. Flexing her knees, she began pumping herself up and down on his cock like a monkey on a stick.

The abrupt change of tactics and technique broke Patterson's concentration and finished him off. Although the weight of her body was nothing, he felt himself go weak at the knees as his balls heaved and his orgasm bubbled up from somewhere deep in the pit of his belly. His swollen cock gave one final explosive throb and then burst like a punctured balloon. He lurched forward, slamming Stella back against the wall bars as he came in a great gush which seemed to drain all energy from his powerful body.

Patterson's vision blurred. He felt as though he was being squeezed out like an old sponge. It was like the woman was sucking his very life-force from his body, he thought dimly, before sinking weakly to the gymnasium floor with a strange roaring sound in his ears.

TWENTY-SIX

EXTRACT FROM *MIAMI HERALD-TRIBUNE*. AUGUST 17TH EDITION.

ONE SIXTY-FIVE EGGHEADS COMING TO TOWN

Miami will be home to some of the nation's most brilliant brains for the next few days as the plush Maison Excalibur Hotel prepares to host the 25th Annual Convention of the One-Sixty-Five Club.

The club, founded in 1972 by the late Professor Marius Zubotsky, is one of the most exclusive organisations in the world, as membership is strictly restricted to people with IQ ratings of 165 or above.

Much of the four-day convention will be given over to an open forum, in which delegates will debate general topics of national and international interest such as Global Pollution and Alternative Energy Sources For The Twenty-First Century.

However, there will also be a series of 'Think-Tanks' in which more specific subjects will be studied in greater detail. Items on this agenda are believed to include National Defence Strategy and Economic Growth Over The Next Two Decades.

Both federal and military representatives are expected to attend the convention, which starts on August 20th.

TWENTY-SEVEN

BUREAU HQ, WASHINGTON, DC. AUGUST 18TH. 9.30 AM.

'You think she's turning homicidal?' Jarvis asked. 'Finally flipped completely?'

Hannah shook his head. 'I think she'd have finished the job off if she meant to kill him. Anyway, Patterson's going to pull through, according to the hospital. Minor heart attack, probably brought on by overexertion. Don't forget the guy had done a two-hour work-out before Stella got to him.'

Jarvis didn't look convinced. 'Overexertion? The guy was a Mr Universe contender for Chrissake.'

Hannah nodded. 'Sure – but they're fragile, these body builders. Their systems are so finely tuned it doesn't take much to knock them right out of kilter. Even a flu bug can floor them, apparently.'

'Acquired medical knowledge?' Jarvis enquired sarcastically.

Hannah looked sheepish. 'Just something I read somewhere.' He was thoughtful for a moment, trying to come up with something which sounded more convincing. 'Anyway, maybe there's a limit to just how much sexual excitement a man can take.'

'Can't be. You're still alive,' Jarvis pointed out cynically. She was silent for a while, becoming serious. 'The point is – she's not just an intriguing little mystery any more. She's dangerous. If she can put an athlete in the intensive care unit, what's she going to do to her next victim if he turns out to have a dicky ticker? We have to track her down and stop her – fast.'

Hannah looked smug. 'Way ahead of you, partner. That's why I've got a plan. Just for once, I figured that thinking with my dick might have a practical application.'

What momentary flash of interest Jarvis might have shown passed away with a resigned sigh. 'This I've got to hear.'

Hannah ignored her, warming to his theme. He spread the map marked with Stella's past travel route out on the desk-top. 'Louisiana was the last stop, right? And we have a report from a gas station attendant in Livingston, Alabama which says a woman answering Stella's description filled up a blue Dodge Dynasty a day later. So we can be pretty sure she's heading back East, and that puts her in striking distance of Florida within the next couple of days.'

Jarvis was looking more interested now. So far, Hannah appeared to be making logic, if not sense. 'So how does that help us track her?' she wanted to know.

Hannah's eyes gleamed. 'Not just track – catch,' he said eagerly. 'We lay a trap.'

He still had her attention so far. Jarvis nodded thoughtfully. 'Alright – how?'

Hannah grinned triumphantly. 'It's all a question of laying the right bait,' he went on. 'My daddy was an ol' Tennessee hunting man. He taught me a thing or two.'

She'd known Hannah long enough to tell the difference between bluster and bullshit. Jarvis's top lip curled disdainfully. 'Hannah, your old man was a New York cab driver who'd sell his grandmother's dentures for a fare as far as the Jersey Tunnel,' she said pointedly.

Hannah wasn't going to be put down, not when he thought he was on a roll. 'Yeah, well – that was my dad by my mum's first marriage,' he said with a shrug. 'Things changed a bit after that.'

Against all her instincts, Jarvis decided to give him the benefit of the doubt. 'OK – so what do we use for this bait?'

'Me,' Hannah said. He sat back in his chair, as though waiting for a round of applause.

It didn't come. Jarvis regarded him with a cold stare. 'And that's your master plan, is it? You come up with yet another little scheme to get yourself laid and I'm supposed to go for it?'

Hannah appeared genuinely hurt. 'Actually, I was thinking of it more in terms of laying down my body in the line of duty.'

He looked quite pitiful. Jarvis decided to give him one last chance. 'Go on,' she muttered wearily.

Hannah brightened at once. 'Look – we know roughly where Stella is, and we know exactly what sort of victim she's going for. What I'm suggesting is that we provide her with a target she can't possibly ignore. Basically, we set her up.'

She was in this deep, she might as well go the whole hog, Jarvis thought. 'How?'

It was time to produce his ace in the hole. Hannah pulled the print-out from the *Miami Herald-Tribune* from his pocket. 'Something I pulled off the Internet,' he explained, handing it to her across the desk. 'I was trying to dig out potential victims that Stella might be tempted to go for, and I hit pay-dirt.'

Jarvis read the cutting through carefully, sucking at her lower lip. Finally, she gave Hannah a little nod. 'Yeah, you could be right,' she conceded. 'An entire hotel-full of the greatest brains makes a pretty fat target.'

'And it's gonna draw Stella like a magnet,' Hannah put in confidently. 'That's if she wasn't already headed there anyway, as her current route would suggest. My guess is that this convention was on her itinerary all along.'

It was more than plausible. It sounded *right*, Jarvis thought. All the same, she tempered her rising enthusiasm with her normal professional caution. 'Only one problem,' she pointed out. 'We don't know which of the delegates she's most likely to go for.'

It was a point Hannah had already considered, and he had an answer all prepared. 'That's what I meant about laying down the right bait. We know that Stella only goes for the top man on the totem pole. So all we have to do is set up a single target who is so clearly head and shoulders above the rest that she won't have any choice.'

This was the one facet of Hannah's plan which Jarvis had so far failed to grasp. 'And that's going to be you?' she asked dubiously.

Hannah nodded. 'Exactly.'

There really wasn't a gentle or diplomatic way of putting it, Jarvis decided, after a few seconds of careful thought. 'Sorry to have to point this out, Hannah,' she muttered finally. 'But another Einstein you definitely are not.'

She had expected him to be upset, but Hannah accepted the put-down with a philosophical shrug. 'So we fake it,' he said simply. 'We've got one of the most efficient disinformation facilities in the world right here in the Bureau. A couple of judicious press releases, a false ID – and I become the Western world's answer to Confucius. Who the hell's going to know the difference? Most of these eggheads talk a load of crap anyway.'

Jarvis thought he was over-simplifying things somewhat, but didn't feel disposed to argue the point. As plans went, it was about all they had and she couldn't come up with anything any better. 'And you think Stella's going to go for it?'

Hannah shrugged. 'Why not? Like I said, she won't have a choice. She'll target me, and I'll grab her. Open and shut.'

'And will this be before or after the big seduction scene?' Jarvis wanted to know.

Hannah feigned innocence. 'I'll just have to play it by ear.'

Jarvis resisted the impulse to enquire whether he was referring to his right ear, his left ear, or the one in his trousers. 'Want me along as back-up?' she asked instead.

'Please yourself,' Hannah said generously. 'But I thought you'd want to follow up on your informant's tip about Walter Jerome. If he's tied into this thing deeper than we originally thought, then we need to know exactly what he was working on before he disappeared.'

He was right, of course, Jarvis realised. Just for once, she got the distinct impression that Hannah was genuinely putting the case before his own interests. She agreed, finally, with a curt nod. 'Well, we'd better get started then, hadn't we? We've only got two days to establish your credentials and cover story.'

TWENTY-EIGHT

HANNAH'S APARTMENT. AUGUST 20TH. 12.55 AM.

The faint snick of the bedroom door opening and closing was followed by a much fainter, almost imperceptible slithering sound.

The sound of a mink coat sliding over smooth flesh on its way to the floor.

Hannah's eyes flickered open. In the semi-darkness, the woman's naked form seemed to glow with a translucent, almost spectral whiteness. Her body was more sensual and more beautiful than he had ever dared to imagine. Pure, raw sex appeal seemed to radiate outwards from her in waves, with an almost animal-like intensity. Besides the tightness in his chest, and the pounding of his heart, Hannah could feel his erection growing.

He found his voice. 'I knew you'd come,' he murmured. 'You want my mind.'

Stella's voice was a low, sexy chuckle. 'But first I want your body.' She glided towards the bed, her lush, full breasts swaying hypnotically. Then she was peeling back the duvet and slipping in beside him.

Hannah's head swam as her warm flesh pressed against his. It was her perfume, he realised dimly. It was a strong, musky smell which he didn't recognise, but which carried the power of a drug. Soporific, intoxicating and aphrodisiac at the same time, it swamped his brain, making him feel completely at the mercy of his own body. There was no way he could resist her, and there was no way he wanted to even try.

She climbed over his prone body, kneeling astride his belly and leaning forwards. Hannah could feel the soft cheeks of her perfect ass pressed against his rising prick, forming a warm and receptive cleft in which it could stiffen and settle. She entwined her slim fingers in the hairs of his chest, gently stroking the contours of his pectoral muscles before finding his nipples. Her breasts dangled invitingly before his eyes.

He had only to raise his head from the pillow to reach them, which Hannah did gratefully. He licked each offered delight in turn, savouring the subtle and delicate contrast between the slight roughness of her erect nipples and the silky smoothness of the surrounding flesh.

Stella sighed, pushing her ass backwards over his now fully stiffened cock. She rose on her knees, holding herself poised above him so that its quivering head rested in the moist crease between her labial lips. She rocked her hips gently from side to side, engaging the domed head of his cock in the warm mouth of her cunt. Then, wriggling sensuously, she lowered herself on to his throbbing shaft.

Hannah's guts tightened as the slippery walls of her pussy engulfed him. He arched his back in an involuntary spasm, driving his proud manhood into the succulent depths of her unbelievably wonderful cunt.

There was no way to describe the ecstatic thrill of sensual pleasure which coursed through his body. Stella felt like no woman he had ever known before, or could possibly ever know again. Sex had always been good – now it was perfect. Her cunt could have been created for his cock alone, designed with precision and loving care for his personal pleasure.

The sensation was so exquisite and so powerful that no man on earth could have fought against it. Hannah did not so much come as feel his juice sucked out of him, syphoned up from his balls and pumped through his twitching cock. He spurted like an erupting volcano, feeling an after-surge of lava-like heat flowing through his loins.

Feeling weak and drained, Hannah looked up at her beautiful face. 'What now?' he breathed.

Stella's limpid blue eyes seemed to glow, suddenly, with the cold, luminous and electrically powered radiance of neon. Her perfect kiss-shaped lips drew back into a bestial snarl, revealing teeth which were no longer white and even. Now they were wolf-like fangs, discoloured and bloodstained. She laughed – but it was a harsh, witch-like cackle. 'Now I suck out your brains,' she grated.

Hannah might have screamed out loud, but he would never know. He awoke then, shivering violently despite the warmth of the duvet. As full consciousness returned, he was uncomfortably aware of the sticky warmth of his discharge inside his pyjamas.

TWENTY-NINE

MAISON EXCALIBUR HOTEL, MIAMI, FLORIDA. AUGUST 20TH. 10.00 AM.

Professor Thomas Hannah, recluse, eccentric expert in the field of quantum physics and the newest member of the One-Sixty-Five Club adjusted his lapel badge and glanced across the hotel lobby. A significant number of his fellow delegates were female, he noted, smiling. What was even more surprising was the number of them which were also highly attractive, rather blowing the widely-held belief that beauty and brains didn't mix.

There were, of course, the expected complement of laboratory mice – all bunned brown hair and horn-rimmed spectacles – along with several frumps in tweed two-pieces and a couple of obvious dykes. But in the main, Hannah was impressed. There were three real stunners among the rest of the contingent, and at least half a dozen others he would be quite happy to share his bed with. If Stella failed to show up, then the four-day convention might not be as boring as he had feared.

In the absence of anyone looking remotely like Stella, Hannah fixed his eyes on a particularly striking redhead. It might pay to stake his claim early, he thought, moving towards her.

He was intercepted halfway across the lobby by a short, but extremely well-proportioned brunette. She grabbed his arm, displaying a remarkably strong grip for such a small woman. Hannah had no time to protest before she pulled him into a quiet corner.

'Well, Professor Hannah. I'm so pleased to meet you. I've read so much about you,' the woman gushed.

Hannah struggled to find a smile, noting out of the corner of his eye that the redhead had already been engaged in conversation by a tall, sun-tanned young man who looked more like a surfer than a scientist. He glanced down at the young woman's lapel badge, identifying her as one Janice Silva. Her face seemed vaguely familiar, he felt, although he couldn't quite place it in context.

'So, Professor – what's your opinion on chaos theory?' Janice demanded.

Hannah had chosen quantum physics as his cover in the fond belief that it was sufficiently esoteric that no one else would know much about it. With a faint sinking feeling, he realised that his present company would appear to have more than a passing acquaintance with the subject. He tried to bluff his way out. 'All very chaotic at present,' he muttered vaguely. 'I shall devote more serious thought to it when they get it sorted out a bit more.'

'And the essential nature of time?' Janice went on. 'Linear, static or accelerative?'

Hannah was way out on a limb now. 'Static?' he ventured nervously. 'But with a tendency towards a slight linear acceleration?'

Janice giggled. 'Hannah, you're not only a fake – you're a goddamned awful fake,' she said quietly. 'How in hell are you going to fool all these super-brains if you can't even fool me?'

Hannah was floored, the smile wiped from his face.

He regarded his inquisitor with a sickly, bemused expression, wishing that the earth would open beneath his feet and swallow him up. 'Excuse me, but what the hell are you talking about?' he managed to croak.

Janice giggled again. She squeezed his arm reassuringly, lowering her voice to a mere whisper. 'Relax, Hannah. Agent Mulholland, Covert Surveillance. But it's still Janice, by the way – just so you don't get too confused.'

The name rang a distinct bell – and suddenly Hannah realised why the woman's face had seemed vaguely familiar. He'd seen her around the Bureau offices – although she was normally a bubbly little blonde, he recalled now. A wig, and a change of make-up was all it took to change her facial appearance, although there was no disguising that pneumatic little figure. He'd quite fancied her, he remembered at the same time. But right now, he was just annoyed.

'What the hell are you doing here?' he demanded. 'Did Jarvis send you to keep tabs on me?'

Janice shook her head. 'Don't overestimate your own importance, Hannah. I'm here to keep an eye on some of the genuine boffins.'

'Then you ought to know better than to approach me so openly,' he muttered irritably. 'You could have blown my cover.'

'You were about to do that yourself. You were making a beeline for the redhead, right?'

'So?'

Janice looked smug. 'CIA. Drafted in specially, all the way from Langley, Virginia. She'd have made you in ten seconds flat – and you know how messy some of these inter-Agency crossovers can get.'

She had a point. Hannah's anger dissipated as he realised that he actually owed her a favour.

'I guess I should thank you,' he muttered contritely.

Janice flashed him a suggestive little smile. 'Actually, I was hoping for a more practical show of gratitude. You can help me win a bet.'

Hannah gaped at her stupidly. 'A bet?'

Janice nodded. 'Nobody in my department's ever laid you. I got fifty bucks riding on me getting to be the first.'

There were worse ways of repaying a favour, Hannah thought. He ran his eyes over Janice's curvy little figure again, finally nodding. 'You got yourself a date. Sometime next week?'

She looked disappointed. 'What's wrong with right now?'

Hannah wasn't often completely thrown, but at this moment he was. He glanced down at his watch. 'It's ten-fifteen in the morning, for Chrissake. We're both supposed to be working undercover.'

Janice shrugged carelessly. 'So we can be working undercover of the bedsheets,' she murmured. 'Unless you're prepared to face the alternative.'

It sounded like a veiled threat. Hannah's eyes narrowed. 'Which is?' he enquired warily.

Janice thrust a copy of the convention agenda under his nose. 'Read that.'

He did. The first item on the day's itinerary was printed in bold type. 'A two-hour Lecture on the Problems of Mass Communication in Underdeveloped Countries, by Dr Lawrence Van Reising.' It sounded dire.

'Or there's me,' Janice said quietly, spelling out his choices.

Hannah cast a quick glance around the hotel lobby. Most of the delegates were already starting to move towards the auditorium. It was decision time. 'Your room or mine?' he asked on impulse.

Janice grinned. 'Mine. Room three five seven,

second floor. And you won't need to bring your notebook.'

Hannah was already backing towards the elevator. 'Give me ten minutes,' he told her.

The door was ajar as Hannah reached Room 357. He walked in, closing it behind him. The bedroom was empty but the sound of a shower running was coming from the adjoining bathroom. Grinning, Hannah kicked off his shoes and padded towards it.

Even through the steam and the frosted glass of the shower cubicle he could appreciate the full lush ripeness of Janice's superb little body. It was a minor miracle of nature that so many curves could be packed into such a small frame. It was definitely a body built for comfort, Hannah told himself, taking in the rounded swell of her hips and ass, the hollowed-out crescent of her back and her tight, pinched little waist. As he watched, Janice bent over to retrieve the tube of shower gel she had just dropped. Her generous breasts hung, pendulously, like two overripe fruits about to drop off the tree. Fruits to be savoured and enjoyed, Hannah thought. He stripped off his clothes hastily, dropping them in an untidy pile on the carpet.

Janice smiled roguishly as he stepped into the shower cubicle beside her. She backed out of the water jet, handing him the shower gel. 'Do me a favour, Hannah,' she pleaded. 'Soap my back for me, will you?'

It wasn't an offer to be refused. Squirting a generous portion of the perfumed goo into one palm, Hannah worked up a rich lather before applying his hands to her smooth shoulders. He worked in a slow, circular motion, enjoying the sensuous delight of his slippery fingers gliding over her silky-smooth flesh.

Janice gave a little shudder of pleasure. 'Ooh, that feels good,' she purred. 'You've got no idea how that pushes my buttons.' She arched her back, pushing her buttocks towards him. 'Do my ass as well, will you?'

It was a tempting prospect, but all in good time, Hannah thought. There was a whole lot of equally attractive territory to be covered on the way. He slipped his hands down from her shoulders and through her armpits, the tips of his fingers tracing out the soft fleshy contours of her tits. Fondling them for a few moments, he moved on, sliding his palms down the flat plane of her belly, over the slicked-down mat of her pubic mound and into the valley between her thighs.

His prick rose of its own accord, settling into the crease between her rounded buttocks. Hannah pushed forward, forcing it between her legs. His fingertips stroked the soft insides of her thighs as he pressed his thumbs together and flicked them gently back and forth against the plump flesh of her labial lips.

Janice groaned softly. She brought her knees together, clamping her thighs tightly around his intruding cock. 'Feel nice?' she murmured.

'Real nice,' Hannah agreed. He started to pull back, trying to work the head of his cock into the mouth of her crack.

Janice turned suddenly, facing him directly. 'Hey,' she chided gently. 'Why the great hurry? We got a couple of hours, remember? I want the rest of the girls to get their fifty bucks worth when I give 'em a full run-through back at the office.'

She stepped back into the main jet of the shower spray, pulling Hannah in with her. He had only a few seconds to appreciate the erotic sight of water droplets bouncing off her stiff little nipples before she sank slowly down to her knees and took his throbbing weapon in her hand, guiding it towards her mouth.

Janice swallowed his cock up to the root, swirling her tongue around the quivering shaft. Then, pulling her head back abruptly, she exposed it to the full pelt of the shower. After the gentle and comforting warmth of her mouth, the sensation of hot water spraying against the sensitive organ was electrifying. Hannah's tool jumped like a galvanised frog, a delicious shiver of pleasure rippling through his entire body. Pleased with his reaction, Janice repeated the manoeuvre a dozen more times, until Hannah was groaning with delirious pleasure. It was an exquisite form of water torture, lifting him to new heights of erotic sensation.

It was also taking him dangerously close to coming and wasting his hot seed into the cascading shower. Hannah reached down and grasped Janice under the armpits, pulling her to her feet. He turned her round, pressing her against the side of the cubicle so that her soft white breasts were squashed against the glass like misshapen blancmanges.

Knowing what was coming, Janice thrust her pert ass outwards in readiness, spreading her legs slightly apart. It was an open invitation, and Hannah accepted it eagerly.

Taking his cock in one hand, he guided it towards its target. Pushing the blunt head into the mouth of her cunt, he rubbed it furiously up and down until it was slick with her juices. Then he lunged forward with his hips, driving the rigid shaft into her smooth and receptive tunnel.

Janice squealed, jerking her ass backwards as his full length plunged into her. Her fingernails raked against the glass wall of the shower cubicle as Hannah pumped himself back and forth, driving his cock in and out of her love-tunnel like a well-greased piston.

Hannah smiled to himself. He had his rhythm going now, and felt in complete control of the situation. The faintly stinging sensation of the power spray on his back was a bonus, acting as a physical and mental distraction to prevent him coming prematurely. With any luck, he felt confident that he could fuck for hours.

But Janice had other ideas. The shower bit had been intended only as a diversion, a titillating little snack before the main course. For that, she wanted Hannah in a nice warm, dry bed – where she could indulge herself in her favourite position of riding on top.

She reached for the shower control, turning it off. Contracting the muscles of her vaginal walls, she squeezed Hannah's imprisoned cock with all her might, rolling her ass around with a gentle circular motion as she did so.

The change of pace broke Hannah's rhythm and his concentration. Struggling to regain both, he jabbed against her ass with feverish contractions of his stomach muscles, but he was fighting a losing battle. The clenching, sucking spasms of Janice's tight little cunt around his shaft had already had their effect. His prick began to throb in response, increasingly violently as his orgasm rose within him.

He surrendered to the inevitable with a final surge of energy, slamming her against the cubicle wall as he pumped himself in and out of her delectable cunt with fast, furious strokes. He came like a hot fountain, with a long, drawn-out sigh of release.

Janice waited until he finally stepped back, letting his softening cock flop out of her wet crack. She pushed her way past him, pulling two soft warm towels off the rack outside the shower and tossing one in his direction.

'Let's hurry up and get dried off,' she called softly, glancing down at her watch by the side of the washbasin. 'We've only got one hour and thirty-three minutes left.'

THIRTY

NASA EXECUTIVE HQ, HOUSTON, TEXAS. AUGUST 22ND. 5.25 PM.

Director Anton Goldsmith was only a small man, but his physical stature was out of all proportion to the size and scope of his position. He sat behind a huge mahogany-topped desk which dwarfed him, even with his swivel chair adjusted to its maximum height. Jarvis found herself reminded of an old science-fiction movie – *The Incredible Shrinking Man* – in which crucial scenes had been shot on a set filled with oversized furniture.

He regarded Jarvis with a wary expression on his face – an expression which had been triggered off by the very mention of Walter Jerome's name.

'Yes, he was a great man,' he muttered abstractedly. 'His loss was a severe blow to us.'

'Do you have any ideas about how or why he might have disappeared?' Jarvis asked directly. 'Theories, even?'

Goldsmith was evasive. 'No – do you?'

Jarvis shook her head. 'That's one of the things we'd like to get cleared up. That, and exactly what projects Jerome was working on at the time.' She waited for an answer to the unspoken question, but none was immediately forthcoming.

Finally, Goldsmith tapped his fingertips together, sucking at his teeth. 'You must realise that information of that nature is on a very top security level,' he said bluntly.

Jarvis nodded. 'Of course – and I have a high enough rating to receive it.'

Goldsmith allowed himself a thin, almost sardonic smile. 'Only just,' he muttered pointedly. 'I'd still be quite within my rights to ask for special clearance from the Pentagon before I gave it to you.' He paused. 'I take it you don't have such clearance?'

It was a direct challenge, but Jarvis didn't flinch. 'I can get it,' she said, with quiet authority. It was a bluff she was hoping Goldsmith would not choose to call, and he didn't.

'Yes, maybe you can,' he agreed. 'And as we're both extremely busy people I can't see that it's worth putting to the test.'

He fell silent again, eyeing her thoughtfully. 'Tell me, Agent Jarvis,' he asked finally, 'how much do you actually understand about the science of cybernetics?'

Jarvis shrugged. 'The study of control and communications systems in machines and living creatures,' she answered, quoting the verbatim dictionary definition she'd looked up before attending the meeting. 'Perhaps more popularly known as AI, or artificial intelligence.'

There was a slightly indulgent smile on Goldsmith's face which fell just short of open condescension. 'You might need to update your reference books, Agent Jarvis,' he told her. 'Things have moved on quite a bit in recent years.'

'And Jerome was in the forefront of such developments?'

Goldsmith shook his head. 'Oh no – Walter Jerome was way out *ahead* of current technology. He was working in the future. Well into the next century, in fact.'

'In the future?' Jarvis repeated, not understanding.

'An extremely long-term project,' Goldsmith confirmed. 'But basically, an integral part of this country's planned colonisation of the planet Mars by the year two thousand and sixty.'

Jarvis was stunned. She whistled under her breath. This was big-league stuff, and it was impossible to think of any conceivable way in which it could tie in with Carl Scheller or Stella Devine.

'It will all be done in stages, of course,' Goldsmith was going on. 'We've already done preliminary surveys, but there will need to be a few more robot probes, reconnaissance and exploration, followed by the first manned landing. Then the real work will begin. Life-supporting bisospheres, water reclamation – and finally the terraforming of the entire planet to make it fit for human habitation. But in between all this, of course, there has to be a vitally important intermediary stage.'

Goldsmith was fishing in his desk as he spoke. 'Here, let me show you something,' he offered, pulling out a single photograph and handing it to Jarvis.

She stared at it – and was unable to resist a little shudder of revulsion. The monstrous, clearly inhuman creature in the picture was an affront to the senses.

'Not pretty, I agree,' Goldsmith murmured, noting her reaction. 'But what you're looking at could be reasonably described as the father, or perhaps the grandfather, of the first true Martian,' he finished off proudly.

Jarvis was having a lot of trouble taking everything in. Even more of a problem was trying to make sense of it, or form any kind of a connection. Unless . . .

As the wildly fanciful, but horrific thought came to her, Jarvis knew that Hannah had to be warned. Her thoughts jumped into overdrive. She grabbed

Goldsmith's phone from his desk without asking, punching out the number of the Maison Excalibur Hotel in Miami.

There was only an unobtainable tone. The hotel's switchboard had been swamped all day by the sheer volume of both inward and outwards calls generated by the convention, and would continue to be so for the rest of the afternoon.

THIRTY-ONE

HANNAH'S HOTEL ROOM. 9.40 PM.

Hannah had retired to his room early, with a six-pack of Bud Ice, a fifth of Old Crow and a video card purchased from the hotel reception desk. One of the cable companies was showing an old Stella Devine movie – *The Baron and the Blonde* – at eleven o'clock, and if the genuine article didn't show up, he was planning to watch it.

More importantly, confining himself to his room would keep him safely out of reach from predatory females. Not content with winning her bet, Janice Mulholland had made it pretty obvious that she was hungry for a rematch. At least three other women delegates had also given him an open come-on over the past forty-eight hours. Having a big brain, it seemed, was almost as good a sexual advertisement as having a big cock.

Under any other circumstances, Hannah would have relished his prospects and made the most of them. The feel of Janice's warm lips wrapped around his stiff cock while the shower beat down on his naked body was still a delicious memory, and something he would love to repeat at some future date. But tonight he needed to save himself for a more important encounter. The last phone call he'd managed to get out of the hotel to

Bureau headquarters had confirmed that Stella had crossed from Alabama into Florida late the previous evening, heading through Pensacola and the Miracle Strip. She was coming for him, Hannah felt sure. It was a gut feeling, a hunch – and it made him feel edgy. The booze helped – although it couldn't quite drive away residual echoes of his previous nightmare.

He lay on the bed, naked, the bottle of bourbon and an opened beer can on the bedside table. The room was oppressively hot. With the hotel fully booked for the convention, the air-conditioning system was as overloaded as the telephone switchboard.

Hannah took a slug of his beer, then checked under his pillow yet again for the comforting feel of the .38 automatic he'd tucked there in readiness. He wasn't convinced that he'd ever be able to use it against a naked and defenceless woman, but it was another legacy of the nightmare.

He sipped at the beer again, waiting.

THIRTY-TWO

SHARK VALLEY, FLORIDA EVERGLADES. 10.09 PM.

Leaving the Interstate had been a mistake, she realised now, although it wasn't really her fault. She should have cut across from Naples to Fort Lauderdale and then picked up the freeway down to Miami. Instead, logic had seemed to dictate that she opt for the shorter route, cutting at least thirty miles off the journey by taking Route 41 directly through the Everglades National Park. And she would always do what was logical.

Except that she hadn't passed an open gas station in over half an hour and the fuel indicator needle had been quivering on zero for the last ten miles of them. The Dodge Dynasty was running on dregs, which wouldn't keep its prodigious thirst at bay for much longer.

As if reading her thoughts, the engine spluttered twice, revved up again momentarily then backfired in the manifold. As it finally died, there was only the hiss of the low-profile tyres against the road as the car rolled slowly to a halt.

Stella switched the ignition off, unconcerned that she was also shutting down the air-conditioning system. She was completely unaffected by the oppressive humidity of the thick, still air. She wound down the side window, equally impervious to the thick swarms of voracious mosquitoes which plagued the surrounding swamplands during the summer months.

She did not even seem unduly concerned about her breakdown, settling back in her seat to listen to the night serenade – the high-pitched chattering of the cicadas playing descant to the belching chorus of several thousand bullfrogs.

She fixed her eyes on the rear-view mirror, preparing to wait. She'd met at least three oncoming vehicles passing through the Miccosukee Indian Reservation and been overtaken twice, so there was still some traffic on the road. It was just a matter of time before someone came along – and she already had an emergency plan in mind.

The wait turned out to be shorter than she had anticipated. Stella saw the distant glow of headlights some two or three miles back down the flat, straight road and swung smoothly into action.

She opened the driver's door, slipping her coat off on to the seat behind her. Stark-naked, she walked out into the middle of the road and stood there, her pale body gleaming in the ghostly light of the half-moon.

'For fuck's sake, Charlie – what the hell is that up ahead?' Jason Twelvetrees screamed. He clawed at his companion's arm. 'Slow down, for Chrissake.'

With one arm draped lazily across the wheel of the Buick pick-up, Charlie Whitefeather raised the half-empty quart bottle of Thunderbird to his lips and took another deep swig. 'Hey, you're having visions, man. Far out.'

Not quite as stoned, Jason strained his eyes as they drew closer. 'No, man – it's a dame, for Chrissake. A dame with no goddamned clothes on.'

Charlie grinned knowingly. 'It's a mirage, man.

Probably swamp gas or somethin'.'

They were less than a hundred yards away now – close enough for Jason to pick out the abandoned Dodge at the side of the road. He yelled again. 'I'm tellin' you that ain't no mirage, man. Hit the brakes, for fuck's sake.'

Charlie got the message at last, remembering at the same time that he was driving his old man's truck, hadn't asked permission and didn't have a valid licence. He stamped on the brake pedal, starting to feel nervous as the gap between the pick-up and Stella continued to close at an alarming rate. 'Why the fuck don't she jump outta the way?' he screamed, panicking.

The Buick slewed to a skidding halt, the front bull-bars only inches from Stella's white thighs. She hadn't even flinched.

In the after-rush of adrenaline hitting the alcohol in his system, Charlie was aggressive. 'What the fuck are you playing at, lady? You trying to get yourself killed?'

Stella walked calmly round the front of the pick-up to the driver's door, wrenching it open. She smiled in at the occupants, apparently unconcerned. 'I need a bit of help, boys. Got any spare gas?'

Charlie's anger melted away as his bleary eyes focused on the full splendour of her naked body, her swelling tits only a few inches from his face. He gulped, licking lips that were dry from the raw alcohol. 'No, we ain't got no gas, lady,' he managed to croak.

Stella accepted this information stoically. 'Then you'll have to give me a lift to the nearest filling station.'

Jason hadn't said anything so far, but now he found his voice. Even in his befuddled state, something told him that a naked female hitchiker alone in the wilderness at night was asking for it. Or if not actually asking for it, offering a fucking good opportunity. Either way, it was worth trying for. 'So what's in it for us, lady?' he asked, suggestively. 'A ride for a ride – know what I mean?'

Stella nodded, her face emotionless. 'You want to fuck me? Fine – only make it quick. I got an appointment.' She backed away a couple of feet. As the two youths piled out, eagerly accepting this unspoken invitation, she stepped round to the rear of the pick-up, hoisting herself up over the open tailgate with her legs dangling over the edge. She spread them apart, resting her heels on the rear licence plate. 'OK, boys – who goes first?'

Quicker on the uptake, Jason was already tugging at his zipper, hoisting out his erect prick. He lurched towards her, holding it in his hand and aiming it drunkenly between her open legs.

She was posed at an ideal height, the crease of her golden-fringed slit a V-shaped shadow against the moonlit whiteness of her smooth thighs. Even in his drunken state, Jason had no difficulty guiding the head of his cock to its target. Waggling it between her soft pussy lips, he bent his knees and thrust his hips forwards.

He groaned with pleasure as the full length of his shaft glided smoothly into the moist warmth of her cunt. He fell forwards over her half-reclined body, pawing at her soft milky breasts with eager fingers. She was one hot piece of ass, he thought briefly, as fluttering soft folds of slippery flesh seemed to close around his cock like a velvet-gloved fist, squeezing and massaging it at the same time. Even stone-cold sober, Jason's sexual technique was sadly inadequate. Lacking both age and experience, he rarely managed to make the sexual act last longer than thirty seconds. Drunk, he couldn't even manage that. He came almost immediately, shooting his hot sauce with a surprised grunt.

Too young to feel embarrassed, he staggered back with a little squeal of triumph. 'Hey, man – I really shot it to that bitch, didn't I?' he bragged to Charlie. 'You wanna grab some of this hot cunt?'

What Charlie wanted, and what he was actually capable of taking, were two completely different things. The youth struggled drunkenly with his zipper, fumbling inside his pants to pull out his pathetically half-flaccid prick. He staggered towards Stella, shaking the useless tool from side to side like a piece of partially defrosted meat. Dimly, he seemed to realise that he wasn't capable of performing even as he approached her.

'Gonna get me a blow job,' he slurred thickly. 'Gonna get some life sucked back into this motherfucker.'

Stumbling, almost falling over, he managed to clamber up into the back of the pick-up, crawling over Stella on his hands and knees. He pressed his groin against her breasts, reaching behind her neck to pull her face down to his drooping cock.

There was a sudden, shrill and blood-curdling scream. Charlie toppled backwards as though he had been struck in the chest by some mighty force. He fell out of the rear of the pick-up, curling up in the road in a near-foetal position, his body contorted with agony. There was a dark red stain spreading rapidly across the front of his pants.

Jason suddenly felt very, very sober. He rushed to his stricken companion, bending over him. His guts churned over. A choked sob rose in his throat.

Stella threw herself off the back of the pick-up, spitting something out of her mouth as she moved. She dashed to the abandoned Dodge, snatching up her coat from the front seat.

She was into the front seat of the Buick and starting

it up before Jason fully realised what was happening. It didn't even seem to matter as the pick-up pulled off, accelerating away up the road. His only concern was for Charlie, still writhing in agony.

His eyes were wide open in horror, rolling wildly. His voice was a whimper, stilted by fear and disbelief.

'She bit the end of my dick off, for Chrissake. The bitch bit my fucking dick off.'

THIRTY-THREE

HANNAH'S HOTEL ROOM. AUGUST 23RD. 12.48 AM.

The credits scrolled upwards off the screen. Hannah cracked open the last of the beers, thumbing the off button on the remote control before the commercials cut in.

There was no doubt that *The Baron and the Blonde* had been one of Stella Devine's greatest movies. In the final wedding scene, she had never looked more radiant, more beautiful or so totally in character.

Hannah sipped at his beer, reflecting that Stella had been a much better actress than many people had given her credit for. In most of her movies, she had portrayed the archetypal sex goddess, and looked every inch the part. But in this role, playing a virginal heroine, she had been equally convincing. It was difficult to imagine that those sweet and gently smiling lips had probably been wrapped around a hundred cocks, that the all-American appeal of that perfect high-school cheerleader's body had been controlled by the mind of a rampant nymphomaniac.

This thought was still in his mind as he heard the faint sound of the doorknob turning. His eyes flickered to the doorway, illuminated in the yellowish glow of the bedside lamp.

Stella wafted, rather than walked, into the room, the

door appearing to close itself behind her. Just as in the Critchlow video, and exactly as her other victims had described it, she was clad in a full-length white mink fur coat, the thick collar pulled up around her neck.

Hannah pushed himself back on his pillow, eyeing her warily and trying to read her face. It was not easy, for the faint smile which curved her luscious lips seemed to barely mask another expression, which was itself yet another mask. Hannah's first impression was that she looked sexy, yet oddly serious at the same time. He corrected it quickly, encapsulating his thoughts into a single word. Enigmatic – that was the way to describe her face.

She took three steps across the room towards the bed and stopped, throwing the mink away behind her with a shrug of her shoulders. She struck a stance, posing for him as a model would pose for the camera, holding her body with a practised professionalism designed to show off every curve with maximum impact. Her soft, kissable lips parted slightly.

'Hello, Professor Hannah.' Her voice was a kittenish purr, low and seductive. 'You know who I am, of course.'

Hannah's face was impassive. 'I know who you *look* like,' he corrected.

Stella tossed her blonde head, dismissively. 'Well, no matter. The important thing is that you know why I'm here. You do know that, don't you?'

So far, Hannah thought, it was running along the general lines of his nightmare. Just for the briefest, fanciful moment, he wondered if it had been a nightmare at all, or some weird kind of premonition.

He ignored her question, asking one of his own instead. 'Why me?'

The enigmatic smile returned. 'I find myself sexually drawn to brilliant men, Professor Hannah. Just as you are sexually drawn to me. Don't I have the most beautiful body you've ever seen?'

Displayed in all its ripe, luscious nakedness, it wasn't something Hannah could argue with, but he tried not to let it show too much. 'And is that all that drives you – just sex?' he demanded.

The smile faded, to be replaced by a peevish frown. 'You ask too many questions. But you *will* give me what I want, I know you will. You already find me impossible to resist.' She paused. 'Look at yourself, Professor, look at your own cock.'

There was a chilling sincerity in her tone. As if hypnotised, Hannah glanced down between his thighs and realised it was true. As if it had a mind of its own, his penis had stiffened into full erection without his being aware of it. Now that he was, the first stirrings of lustful desire began to quiver in his belly.

His surprise must have shown on his face. Stella gave a gloating chuckle. 'What is it that you find so hard to accept or understand, Professor? That all you men are so stupidly weak? That even a brain such as yours is completely at the mercy of that pathetic piece of flesh you have between your legs?'

It made no kind of sense at all, Hannah thought. This encounter was turning out in a way he would never have imagined. Based on the Critchlow video and the personal accounts of her other victims, he had assumed Stella to be so devastatingly and overpoweringly sensual that she was sexually irresistible.

But this was not a seduction – it was a duel. She was openly mocking him, insulting his manhood. Doing everything, in fact, that should have been a complete and utter turn-off.

Yet his cock was throbbing more urgently than ever. Despite himself, Hannah wanted her more than any other woman he had ever seen. His desire was almost a pain. He wondered, briefly, whether she was exercising some kind of hypnotism or mind control. Or perhaps she was exuding raw pheremones which acted directly on his central nervous system.

Either way, he knew that she had spoken the truth. He would be totally incapable of resisting her. Strangely, this realisation triggered a wave of relief which washed over his body and brain. It felt good, suddenly, that he didn't have to fight anymore. That he could just give in, abandon himself to the promised delights of her unbelievably sensual body and enjoy the erotic experience of his life.

Stella seemed to understand, instinctively, that she had won. She smiled triumphantly. 'Now let's stop the talking, shall we? Let's get down to what we both really want.'

She moved across to the side of the bed, standing over him. She reached down, cradling his stiff flesh in her fingers and stroking it gently. Hannah shivered with pleasure at her touch. Pulling himself into a sitting position against the bed's headboard, he gazed up at the flawless perfection of her beautiful body.

It was almost *too* perfect, he found himself thinking. There was something not quite right, something which niggled at the back of his mind. He reached up, stroking one fingertip down over the proud curvature of her magnificent breasts with a sense of wonder.

Suddenly, it came to him. With no apparent break in the heatwave of the past few days, the room was still insufferably humid. Yet there wasn't the faintest trace of perspiration on Stella's body. Her skin felt cool and dry to the touch. Like a snake's, he reflected.

The thought faded from his mind as quickly as it had surfaced. It didn't seem important, somehow. She was bending over him now, letting her delicious tits swing enticingly in front of his eyes. The overpowering need to fondle them, to suck upon her sweet and fruit-like nipples swamped his senses.

Hannah reached for them like a hungry infant. Grasping the two mounds of swelling flesh in his hands, he pulled them towards his face, straining to plunge his mouth over the nearest coral-pink delight. His lips closed over their target. Making little grunting noises, he worked the firm little bud with his teeth and tongue.

Stella clambered on the bed, throwing one knee over his hips. She reached for his stiff prick, curling her fingers around the throbbing shaft and guiding it between her thighs. Hannah shuddered as she rubbed the sensitive head against the knob of her clitoris, working it well into the warm slit between her pussy lips. Like the petals of a flower welcoming a pollinating bee, her cunt seemed to open up to receive it.

As she sank down on him, Hannah felt his own hardness engulfed by her slippery softness, and the sensation was so intensely pleasurable that it almost took his breath away. With a grunt, he thrust upward, wanting to bury his entire being inside her. His cock plunged into her depths until their pelvises ground against each other, preventing further penetration. There was little more he could do except rock his hips from side to side, making his prick vibrate inside her enclosing love-tunnel.

Completely filled with his manhood, Stella dropped her full body weight upon him. She began to grind her pelvis around in small circles, pumping back and forth with her hips and stomach with short, jabbing strokes. Hannah's eyes rolled from side to side distractedly. He clamped his hands around her beautifully rounded buttocks, his fingernails digging into the firm flesh like talons, not caring whether he hurt her or not. He was so completely immersed in the savage intensity of his own pleasure that nothing else seemed to matter. Not Stella – not even himself. He could only ride the sexual ecstasy of the moment, knowing that it could not last for much longer. His prick was bursting, his balls tingling like they'd been wired up to an electric shock machine.

He screamed as his orgasm broke, feeling himself spurt out like a fractured hot water faucet.

Stella ground herself down on to him one last time, flexing inner muscles which made the walls of her cunt contract around his cock like a gloved fist. She sat upright, pinched her finger and thumb around the base of his wilting tool and squeezed it out as she lifted herself off his body. She said nothing, but there was a faint smile of satisfaction playing over her delicious lips.

Hannah flopped back against the pillows as she swung herself over to the edge of the bed and stood up, heading straight into the bathroom. He waited to hear the sound of running water, or the toilet flushing – but there was only a long silence.

Curious, he forced his weak body off the bed and followed her, pushing open the bathroom door which she had closed, but not locked. He'd been prepared for embarrassment, but not the bizarre sight which greeted him.

Stella was kneeling on the floor with her legs spread wide apart, her ass pressed against her heels and her upper torso arched back. One hand was thrust up her cunt as far as the wrist. She looked up in shock, her face flashing alarm as Hannah stepped in, but it was already too late to stop the process she had initiated.

There was a faint click, followed by a whirring sound. Hannah's eyes widened in disbelief as a whole section of her belly from her navel down swung open like a trapdoor, revealing the silvery gleam of metal where her guts ought to have been.

Shock and horror temporarily numbed his otherwise lightning reflexes. Hannah reeled back against the bathroom wall, gaping impotently as Stella suddenly launched herself up from the floor with inhuman strength and speed. She was upon him before he could do anything about it, jabbing her index finger against his chest, just below the heart.

There was a momentary sensation of heat, then of pain – and then nothing. Blackness closed in on Hannah's mind as he collapsed, sliding down the wall like a punctured blow-up doll.

Consciousness came like a train emerging from a long and dark tunnel. There was a roaring sound in his ears, a throbbing pain in his chest, and every muscle in his body seemed to ache. Hannah pulled himself to his feet with an effort, bracing his back against the wall because he wasn't sure whether his groggy legs could support the weight of his body.

They could – just. Hannah leaned against the wall for a long time, trying to get his strength back and his thoughts together. He had no idea how long he'd been out, but it was daylight. Finally, he regained his senses enough to glance down at his wristwatch. It was just after 10.30 in the morning. He was also suddenly aware that the room felt much cooler, even though the air-conditioning system had been completely switched off. After the heatwave of the past few days, a temperature inversion like that in Florida could only mean one thing, he realised. There was a major storm front on its way.

He felt strong enough to try walking now. Hannah pushed himself away from the wall, testing his legs. They felt wobbly, but he thought he could make it.

His eyes caught the silvery gleam of a small metal

canister, about the size of a disposable lighter, laying on the bathroom floor. He stooped to pick it up, dropping it again almost immediately. It was icy-cold to the touch, stinging his fingers. He pulled a dozen sheets of toilet tissue from the dispenser, wrapping it up and carrying it into the bedroom. He dressed as quickly as he could, stuffing the canister into the top pocket of his jacket.

Downstairs, the hotel lobby was completely deserted. Behind the reception desk, instead of a clerk, stood a fully-uniformed National Guardsman. He glared at Hannah with a mixture of exasperation and anger. 'Where the fuck have you been for the last two hours? Didn't you hear the hotel fire alarm, for Chrissake?'

Hannah regarded him blankly. 'There's been a fire?'

The guard rolled his eyes, delivering his message in verbal shorthand. 'Hurricane blowing in from the Azores. Big one. Standard evacuation procedure. Head inland. Your nearest emergency centre will be the Lake Obeechobee ranger station out on Route twenty-seven.'

Hannah pulled his ID. 'Thanks, but I've got to get to Washington as fast as possible. Anything still flying out of Miami International?'

The young man was immediately more deferential. Even in an emergency, the Bureau still outranked the National Guard. 'There'll still be some military transport. I'll call in a chopper to pick you up.' He paused, grinning. 'That musta been one hell of a night you had yourself there, feller.'

Hannah nodded – and immediately wished he hadn't. 'Yeah, one hell of a night,' he agreed weakly.

THIRTY-FOUR

MOUNTJOY MILITARY HOSPITAL, WASHINGTON, DC.
AUGUST 25TH. 11.42 AM.

'You've got visitors,' the pretty blonde nurse announced.

Hannah propped himself up in bed as Jarvis and Stone walked into the private room. Jarvis had a bunch of grapes, but he would have preferred them already fermented and bottled.

'Is he fit to talk?' Stone asked the nurse.

She snorted. 'I'd say he's fit for anything. He's tried to goose me twice this morning already.' With a toss of her blonde head, she flounced off, leaving them alone.

Stone turned to Hannah. 'Well, welcome back to the land of the living. We had a few doubts over the last couple of days.'

Hannah looked blank. The last thing he could actually remember clearly was feeling giddy in the helicopter.

Jarvis filled in the gaps. 'Whatever she zapped you with, it was pretty potent. You've been in and out of coma for over forty-eight hours.'

It was all starting to come back now. He clutched at Jarvis's hand. 'Stella wasn't human,' he blurted out, urgently. 'She was some kind of robot.'

Jarvis nodded. 'Android,' she corrected. 'A combination of mechanical body parts and laboratory-cultured human tissue. That was what Walter Jerome was working on at NASA. Something which could live and work on Mars until there were enough biospheres to support human colonists.'

Hannah hardly took it in. There were too many other mysteries, things he still didn't understand. 'The capsule. Did you analyse the capsule?'

Jarvis nodded again. 'A sample of human semen, cryogenically frozen in liquid nitrogen.' She read the unspoken question in his eyes. 'Oh, not yours – we already had your DNA record on file. It fitted the pattern for an Afro-American, so it was probably Patterson's.'

'And Stella?' Hannah wanted to know. 'Did she get away?'

'She hired a power boat at North Beach,' Stone told him. 'Last seen heading straight out to sea towards the coordinates where Scheller vanished.'

'And smack into the middle of the Bermuda Triangle,' Hannah pointed out.

Stone looked uncomfortable. The mere mention of the Bermuda Triangle had been enough to put his guard up. He shrugged the observation off, not wanting to encourage Hannah in another one of his wild theories. 'Wherever she was headed, it's unlikely she made it. That course would have taken her right into the path of Hurricane Wilbur, and it was a real mean bastard.' He broke off to glance at his watch. 'Well, I'll leave you two together to compare notes. I'll expect your preliminary report on my desk by noon tomorrow.'

'He doesn't want the truth,' Hannah said quietly after Stone had left the room. 'He wants a whitewash, another Sex File packed away in a brown manilla envelope and locked up in the basement.'

Jarvis hunched her shoulders. 'So what's the truth,

Hannah? Stella's gone, and what have we actually got?'

'Enough to know that we're dealing with an extraterrestrial intelligence here,' he said calmly. 'You must have seen some up-to-date reports on Jerome's work while you were at NASA. Was he capable of building anything as sophisticated as Stella?'

He had a point. 'No, probably not,' she had to admit.

'Then we're talking about a vastly superior technology,' Hannah went on, getting into his stride. 'But they needed a human brain to design the basic framework, so they abducted Walter Jerome to build it. Then Carl Scheller to give it a convincing human body and face. But because of his obsession, he seized the opportunity to create another Stella Devine.'

Jarvis's brain was swimming. 'And who are *they*, Hannah?'

'Whatever – or whoever – are out there in the Triangle. With the technology and the power to interfere with the very Earth's electro-magnetic field, to cause freak storms or tidal waves, to make boats, nuclear submarines and even entire squadrons of planes disappear without a single trace of debris or a human survivor ever being found.'

'But why? To what purpose?'

Hannah didn't have an answer. Just theories. 'Stella was collecting human sperm samples,' he pointed out. 'From the cream of American manhood. Perhaps they possess cloning techniques way ahead of ours. Maybe they want to breed their own humans for some purpose. It could simply be a more efficient way of obtaining experimental subjects without having to abduct whole people. Or maybe they plan to produce a super-human by combining all the samples together. Imagine it, Jarvis. The brightest, fastest, strongest, fittest and most ruthlessly aggressive human being there ever was.'

It was all too much to take in. Jarvis sought mental release, finding it in humour. She began to chuckle – at first to herself and finally openly.

'Then God help them, and God knows what they're going to produce,' she said to Hannah, who was scowling at her. 'The poor bastards haven't got the faintest idea that they've got your sperm mixed up in their little melting pot.'

It took Hannah a long time to appreciate the joke, but he finally joined in with the merriment – at least as much as his still-aching body would allow.